THE GOSPEL IN BRIEF

LEO TOLSTOY

TRANSLATED BY AYLMER MAUDE

British Library Cataloguing in Publication Data

A catalogue record for this book is available from the British Library

ISBN-13: 978-1-911405-11-5

Cover Illustration: *Jesus Washing Peter's Feet*
Ford Madox Brown (1852-56)

CONTENTS

Everything which I teach men to do
is easy and simple,
for the Kingdom of God
is announced as bliss.

Author's Preface

This short exposition of the Gospel is a summary of a large work which exists in manuscript and cannot be published in Russia.

That work consists of four parts:

1. An account (Confession) of the course of my own life and of the thoughts which led me to the conviction that the Christian teaching contains the truth.

2. An examination of the Christian teaching: first according to its interpretation by the Orthodox Russo-Greek Church, then according to its interpretation by the Church in general - by the Apostles, the Councils, the so-called Fathers of the Church - and an exposure of what is false in those interpretations.

3. An examination of Christian teaching not according to those interpretations but solely according to what has come down to us of Christ's teaching, as ascribed to him in the Gospels.

4. An exposition of the real meaning of Christ's teaching, the reasons why it has been perverted, and, the consequences to which it should lead.

From the third of those parts the present account as been compiled.

The harmonization of the four Gospels has been in accord with the sense of the teaching. In making it I hardly had to digress from the order in it is set down in the Gospels, so that there are not more but fewer transpositions of the verses than in most of the concordances known to me, or than in Grechulevich's arrangement of the Four Gospels. In my treatment of the Gospel of John there are no transpositions, but everything follows the order of the original.

The division of the Gospel into twelve chapters (or six if each two be united) came about of itself from the sense of the teaching. This is the meaning of those chapters:

1. Man is the son of an infinite source: a son of that Father not by the flesh but by the spirit.
2. Therefore man should serve that source in spirit.
3. The life of all men has a divine origin. It alone is holy.
4. Therefore man should serve that source in the life of all men. Such is the will of the Father.
5. The service of the will of that Father of life gives life.
6. Therefore the gratification of one's own will is not necessary for life.
7. Temporal life is food for the true life.
8. Therefore the true life is independent of time: it is in the present.
9. Time is an illusion of life; life in the past and in the future conceals from men the true life of the present.
10. Therefore man should strive to destroy the illusion of the temporal life of the past and future.

11. True life is life in the present, common to all men and manifesting itself in love.

12. Therefore, he who lives by love in the present, through the common life of all men, unites with the Father, the source and foundation of life.

So each two chapters are related as cause and effect

In addition to these twelve chapters an introduction from the first chapter of the Gospel of John is added, in which the writer of that Gospel speaks, in his own name, as to the meaning of the whole teaching, and a conclusion from the same writer's Epistle (written probably before the Gospel) containing a general deduction from all that precedes.

These two parts do not form an essential part of the teaching, but though they both might be omitted without losing the sense of the teaching (the more so as they come in the name of John and not of Jesus) I have retained them because in a straightforward understanding of Christ's teaching these parts, confirming one another and the whole, furnish, in contradiction to the queer interpretation of the Churches, the plainest indication of the meaning that should be ascribed to the teaching.

At the beginning of each chapter, besides a brief indication of its subject, I have given the words which correspond to that chapter from the prayer Jesus taught his disciples.

When I had finished my work I found to my surprise and joy that the Lord's Prayer is nothing but a very concise expression of the whole teaching of Jesus in the very order in which I had arranged the chapters, and that each phrase of the prayer corresponds to the meaning and sequence of the chapters:

1.	Our Father,	Man is a son of God
2.	Which art in Heaven,	God is the infinite spiritual source of life.
3.	Hallowed be Thy Name,	May this source of life be held holy
4.	Thy Kingdom come,	May his power be realized in all men
5.	Thy will be done, as in heaven,	May His will be fulfilled as it is in himself
6.	So also on earth,	so also in the bodily life.
7.	Give us our daily bread,	Temporal life is the food of the true life.
8.	This day.	True life is in the present.
9.	And forgive us our debts as we forgive our debtors,	And let not the mistakes and errors of the past hide that true life from us.
10.	And lead us not into temptation,	And may they not lead us into delusion,
11.	But deliver us from evil,	And so there shall be no evil.
12.	For thine is the kingdom the power, and the glory,	And may thy power, and strength, and wisdom, prevail.

In the full exposition, in the third part, everything in the Gospels is set down without any omissions. But in the present rendering the following are omitted: the conception and birth of John the Baptist, his imprisonment and death, the birth of Jesus, his genealogy, his mother's flight with him to Egypt; his miracles at Cana and Caperaum; the casting out of the devils; the walking on the sea; the blasting of the fig-tree; the healing of the sick; the raising of the dead; the resurrection of Christ himself, and the references to prophecies fulfilled by his life.

Those passages are omitted in the present short exposition because, containing nothing of the teaching but only describing events that took place before, during, or after the period in which Jesus taught, they complicate the exposition. Those verses, however they may be understood, do not contain either contradiction or confirmation of the teaching. Their sole significance for Christianity was to prove the divinity of Jesus to those who did not believe in it. But for one who understands that a story of miracles is unconvincing, and who also doubts that the divinity of Jesus is asserted in his teaching, those verses drop away of themselves as superfluous.

In the larger work every deviation from the ordinary version, as well as every inserted comment and every omission, is explained and justified by comparison of the different variants of the Gospels, by examination of contexts, and by philological and other considerations. In the present brief rendering all such proofs and refutations of the false understanding of the Churches, as well as the detailed notes and references, are omitted, on the ground that however exact and correct the discussions of each separate passage may be, they cannot carry conviction as to the true understanding of the teaching. The justness of the understanding of the teaching is better proved not by the discussion of particular passages but by its own unity, clarity, simplicity and completeness, and by its accordance with the inner feeling of all who seek the truth.

In respect of all the divergences of my rendering from the Church's authorized text, the reader should not forget that the customary conception that the four Gospels with all their verses and syllables are sacred books is a very gross error.

The reader should remember that Jesus never wrote any book himself, as Plato, Philo, or Marcus Aurelius did; nor even, like Socrates, transmitted his teaching to educated men, but that he spoke to many uneducated men and only long after his death did people begin to write down what they had heard about him.

The reader should remember that there were very many such accounts from among which the Churches selected first three Gospels and then one more, and that in selecting those best Gospels as the proverb, - 'There is no stick without knots' says - they had to take in many knots with what they selected from the whole mass of writings about Christ, and that there are many passages in the canonical Gospels just as poor as in the rejected apocryphal ones.

The reader should remember that it is the teaching of Christ which may be sacred, but certainly not any definite number of verses and syllables, and that certain verses picked out from here to there cannot become sacred merely because people say they are.

Moreover the reader should remember that these selected Gospels are also the work of thousands of different human brains and hands, that they have been selected, added to, and commented on, for centuries, that all the copies that have come down to us from the fourth century are written in continuous script without punctuation, so that even after the fourth and fifth centuries they have been subject to very diverse readings, and that there are not less than fifty thousand such variations of the Gospels.

This should all be borne in mind by the reader, that he may not be misled by the customary view that the Gospels in their present form have come to us direct from the Holy Ghost.

The reader should remember that far from it being blameworthy to discard useless passages from the Gospels and elucidate some passages by others, it is on the contrary irrational not to do so and to hold a certain number of verses and syllables as sacred.

On the other hand I beg readers to remember that if I do not regard the Gospels as sacred books that have come down to us from the Holy Ghost, even less do I regard them as mere historical monuments of religious literature. I understand the theological as well as the historical view of the Gospels, but regard them myself differently, and so I beg the reader not to be confused either by the church view or by the historical view customary today among educated people, neither of which I hold.

I regard Christianity neither as an inclusive divine revelation nor as an historical phenomenon, but as a teaching which gives us the meaning of life. I was led to Christianity neither by theological nor historical investigations but by this - that when I was fifty years old, having asked myself and all the learned men around me what I am and what is the meaning of my life, and received the answer that I am a fortuitous concatenation of atoms and that life has no meaning but is itself an evil, I fell into despair and wanted to put an end to my life; but remembered that formerly in childhood when I believed, life had a meaning for me, and that for the great mass of men about me who believe and are not corrupted by riches life has a meaning; and I doubted the validity of the reply given me by the learned men of my circle and I tried to understand the reply Christianity gives to those who live a real life. And I began to seek Christianity in the Christian teaching that guides such men's lives. I began to study the Christianity which I saw applied in life and to compare that applied Christianity with its source.

The source of Christian teaching is the Gospels, and in them I found the explanation of the spirit which guides the life of all who really live.

But together with this source of the pure water of life I found, wrongfully united with it, mud and slime which had hidden its purity from me: by the side of and bound up with the lofty Christian teaching I found a Hebrew and a Church teaching alien to it. I was in the position of a man who receives a bag of stinking dirt, and only after long struggle and much labor finds that amid that dirt lie priceless pearls; and he understands that he was not to blame for disliking the stinking dirt, and that those who have collected and preserved these pearls together with the dirt are also not to blame but deserve love and respect.

I did not know the light and had thought there was no light of truth to be found in life, but having convinced myself that men live by that light alone, I began to look for its source and found it in the Gospels, despite the false Church interpretations. And on reaching that source of light I was dazzled by it, and found full replies to my questions as to the meaning of my own life and that of others - answers in full agreement with those I knew of from other nations, but which in my opinion were superior to them all.

I was looking for an answer to the question of life and not to theological or historical questions, and so for me the chief question was not whether Jesus was or was not God, or from whom the Holy Ghost proceeded and so forth, and equally unimportant and unnecessary was it for me to know when and by whom each Gospel was written and whether such and such a parable may, or may not, be ascribed to Christ. What was important to me was this light which has enlightened mankind for eighteen hundred years and which enlightened and still enlightens me; but how to name the source of that light, and what materials he or someone else had kindled, did not concern me.

On that, this preface might end were the Gospels recently discovered books and had Christ's teaching not suffered eighteen hundred years of false interpretation. But now to understand the teaching of Jesus it is necessary to know clearly the chief methods used in these false interpretations. The most customary method of false interpretation, and one which we have grown up with, consists of preaching under the name of Christianity not what Christ taught but a church teaching composed of explanations of very contradictory writings into which Christ's teaching enters only to a small degree, and even then distorted and twisted to fit together with other writings. According to this false interpretation Christ's teaching is only one link in a chain of revelations beginning with the commencement of the world and continuing in the Church until now. These false interpreters call Jesus God; but the fact that they recognize him as God does not make them attribute more importance to his words and teaching than to the words of the Pentateuch, the Psalms, the Acts of the Apostles, the Epistles, the Apocalypse, or even to the decisions of the Councils and the writings of the Fathers of the Church.

These false interpreters do not admit any understanding of the teaching of Jesus which does not conform to the previous and subsequent revelations; so that their aim is not to explain the meaning of Christ's teaching, but as far as possible to harmonize various extremely contradictory writings, such as the Pentateuch, the Psalms, the Gospels, the Epistles, and the Acts - that is, all that is supposed to constitute the Holy Scriptures.

Such explanations aiming not at truth but at reconciling the irreconcilable, namely, the writings of the Old and the New Testament, can obviously be innumerable, as indeed they are. Among them are the Epistles of Paul and the decisions of the Councils (which begin with the formulary: 'It has pleased Us and the Holy Ghost'), and such enactments as those of the Popes, the Synods, the pseudo-Christs, and all the false interpreters who affirm that the Holy Ghost speaks through their lips. They all employ one and the same gross method of affirming the truth of their interpretations by the assertion that their interpretations are not human utterances but revelations from the Holy Ghost. Without entering on an examination of these beliefs, each of which calls itself the true one, one cannot help seeing that by the method common to them all of acknowledging the whole immense quantity of so-called scriptures of the Old and New Testament as equally sacred, they themselves impose an insuperable obstacle to an understanding of Christ's teaching; and that from this mistake arises the possibility and inevitability of endlessly divergent interpretations of the teaching. The reconcilement of a number of revelations can be infinitely varied, but the interpretation of the teaching of one person (and one looked upon as God) should not occasion discord.

If God descended to earth to teach people, his teaching, by the very purpose of his coming, cannot be understood in more than one way. If God came down to earth to reveal truth to men, at least he would have revealed it so that all might understand: if he did not do that he was not God; and if the divine truths are such that even God could not make them intelligible to mankind, men certainly cannot do so.

If Jesus is not God, but a great man, then still less can his teaching produce discord. For the teaching of a great man is only great because it expresses intelligibly and clearly what others have expressed unintelligibly and obscurely. What is incomprehensible in a great man's teaching is not great, and therefore a great man's teaching does not engender sects. Only an exposition which affirms that it is a revelation from the Holy Ghost and is the sole truth, and that all other expositions are lies, gives birth to discord and to the mutual animosities among the Churches that result therefrom. However much the various Churches affirm that they do not condemn other communities, that they have no hatred of them but pray for union, it is untrue. Never, since the time of Arius, has the affirmation of any dogma arisen from any other cause than the desire to condemn a contrary belief as false. It is a supreme degree of pride and ill will to others to assert that a particular dogma is a divine revelation proceeding from the Holy Ghost: the highest presumption because nothing more arrogant can be said than that the words spoken by me are uttered through me by God; and the greatest ill will because the avowal of oneself as in possession of the sole indubitable truth implies an assertion of the falsity of all who disagree. Yet that is just what all the Churches say, and from this alone flows and has flowed all the evil which has been committed and still is committed in the world in the name of religion.

But besides the temporary evil which such an interpretation by the Churches and the sects produces, it has another important inner defect which gives an obscure, indefinite, and insincere character to their assertions. This defect consists in the fact that all the Churches - having acknowledged the latest revelation of the Holy Ghost, who descended on the apostles and has passed and still passes to the supposedly elect - nowhere define directly, definitely, and finally, in what that revelation consists; and yet they base their belief on that supposedly continuing revelation and call it Christian. All the churchmen who acknowledge the revelation from the Holy Ghost recognize (like the Mohammedans) three revelations: that of Moses, of Jesus, and of the Holy Ghost. But in the Mohammedan religion it is believed that after Moses and Jesus, Mahomet is the last of the prophets and that he explained the revelations of Moses and Jesus, and this revelation of Mahomet every True Believer has before him.

But it is not so with the Church faith. That also, like the Mohammedan, acknowledges three revelations: that of Moses, of Jesus, and of the Holy Ghost, but it does not call itself Holy Ghostism after the name of the last revealer, but affirms that the basis of its faith is the teaching of Christ. So that while preaching, its own doctrines it attributes their authority to Christ. Churchmen acknowledging the last revelation explaining all previous ones, should say so and call their religion by the name of whoever received the last revelation - acknowledging it to be that of Paul, or of this or that Council of the Church, or of the Pope, or of the Patriarch. And if the last revelation was that of the Fathers, a decree of the Eastern Patriarchs, a Papal encyclical, or the syllabus or catechism of Luther or of Philaret - they should say so and call their religion accordingly, because the last revelation which explains all the preceding is always the most important one. But they do not do so, but while preaching doctrines quite alien to Christ's teaching, affirm that their doctrine was taught by Christ. So that according to their teaching Jesus declared that by his blood he had redeemed the human race ruined by Adam's sins; that God is three persons; that the Holy Ghost descended upon the apostles and was transmitted to the priesthood by the laying on of hands; that seven sacraments are necessary for salvation; that communion should be received in two kinds, and so on. They would have us believe that all this is the teaching of Jesus, whereas in reality there is not a word about any of it in his teaching. Those false teachers should call their teaching and religion the teaching, and religion of the Holy Ghost but not of Christ; for only that faith can be called Christian which recognizes the revelation of Christ reaching us in the Gospels as the final revelation.

It would seem that the matter is plain and not worth speaking about, but, strange to say, up to now the teaching of Christ is not separated on the one side from an artificial and quite unjustifiable amalgamation with the Old Testament, and on the other from the arbitrary additions and perversions made in the name of the Holy Ghost.

To this day there are some who, calling Jesus the second person of the Trinity, do not conceive of his teaching otherwise than in conjunction with those pseudo revelations of the third Person which they find in the Old Testament, the Epistles, the decrees of the Councils and the decisions of the Fathers, and they preach the strangest beliefs, affirming them to be the religion of Christ.

Others not acknowledging Jesus as God, similarly conceive of his teaching not as he could have taught it but as understood by Paul and other commentators. While regarding Jesus not as God but as a man, these commentators deny him a most legitimate human right, that of answering only for his own words and not for false interpretations of them. Trying to explain his teaching, these learned commentators attribute to Jesus things he never thought of saying. The representatives of this school of interpreters - beginning with the most popular of them, Renan - without troubling to separate what Jesus himself taught from what the slanders of his commentators have laid upon him, and without troubling to understand his teaching more profoundly, try to understand the meaning of his appearance and the spread of his teaching by, the events of his life a and the circumstances of his time.

The problem that confronts them is this: eighteen hundred years ago a certain pauper appeared and said certain things. He was flogged and executed. And ever since that time (though there have been numbers of just men who died for their faith), milliards of people, wise and foolish, learned and ignorant, have clung to the belief that this man alone among men was God. How is this amazing fact to be explained? The churchmen say that it occurred because Jesus was God. In that case it is all understandable. But if he was not God how are we to explain that everyone looked upon just this common man as God? And the learned men of that school assiduously explore every detail of the life of Jesus, without noticing that however much they explore those details (in reality they have gathered none), even if they were able to reconstruct his whole life in the minutist detail, the question why he, just he, had such an influence on people would still remain unanswered. The answer is not to be found in knowledge of the society Jesus was born into, or how he was educated, and so on, still less is it to be found in knowledge of what was being done in Rome, or in the fact that the people of that time were inclined to superstition, but only by knowing what this man preached that has caused people, from that time to this, to distinguish him from all others and to acknowledge him as God. It would seem that the first thing to do is to try to understand that man's teaching, and naturally his own teaching and not coarse interpretations of it that have been spread since his time. But this is not done. These learned historians of Christianity are so pleased to have understood that Jesus was not God and are so anxious to prove that his teaching is not divine and is therefore not obligatory, that forgetting that the more they prove him to have been an ordinary man and his teaching not to be divine the further they are from solving the problem before them - they strain all their strength to do so. To see this surprising error clearly, it is worth recalling an article by Havet, a follower of Renan's, who affirms that Jesus Christ *n'avait rien de chrétien*, or Souris, who enthusiastically argues that Jesus Christ was a very coarse and stupid man.

The essential thing is, not to prove that Jesus was not God and that therefore his doctrine is not divine, or to prove that he was a Catholic, but to know in all its purity what constituted that which was so lofty and so precious to men that they have acknowledged and still acknowledge its preacher to have been God.

And so if the reader belongs to the great majority of educated people brought up in the Church belief but who have abandoned its incompatibilities with common sense and conscience - whether he has retained a love and respect for the spirit of the Christian teaching or (as the proverb puts it: 'has thrown his fur coat into the fire because he is angry with the bugs') considers all Christianity a harmful superstition - I ask him to remember that what repels him and seems to him a superstition is not the teaching of Christ; that Christ cannot be held responsible for that monstrous tradition that has been interwoven with his teaching and presented as Christianity: that to prejudge of Christianity, on the teaching of Christ as it has come down to us must be learned - that is, the words and actions attributed to Christ and that have an instructive meaning. Studying the teaching of Christ in that way the reader will convince himself that Christianity, far from being a mixture of the lofty and the low, or a superstition, is a very strict, pure, and complete metaphysical and ethical doctrine, higher than which the reason of man has not yet reached, and in the orbit of which (without recognizing the fact) human activity - political, learned, poetic, and philosophic - is moving.

If the reader belongs to that small minority of educated people who hold to the Church religion and profess it not for outward purposes but for inward tranquillity, I ask him to remember that the teaching of Christ as set forth in this book (despite the identity of name) is quite a different teaching from that which he professes, and that therefore the question for him is not whether the doctrine here offered agrees or disagrees with his belief, but is simply, which best accords with his reason and conscience - the Church teaching composed of adjustments of many scriptures, or the teaching of Christ alone? The question for him is merely whether he wishes to accept the new teaching or to retain his own belief.

But if the reader is one of those who outwardly profess the Church creed and values it not because he believes it to be true but because he considers that to profess and preach it is profitable to him, then let him remember that however many adherents he may have, however powerful they may be, on whatever thrones they may sit, and by whatever great names they may call themselves, he is not one of the accusers but of the accused. Let such readers remember that there is nothing for them to prove, that they have long ago said what they had to say and that even if they could prove what they wish to, they would only prove, each for himself, what is proved by all the hundreds of opposing Churches; and that it is not for them to demonstrate, but to excuse themselves: to excuse themselves for the blasphemy of adjusting the teaching of the God-Christ to suit the teaching of Ezras, of the Councils, and Theophilacts, and allowing themselves to interpret and alter the words of God in conformity with the words of men; to excuse themselves for their libels on God by which they have thrown all the fanaticism they had in their hearts onto the God-Jesus and given it out as his teaching; to excuse themselves for the fraud by which, having hidden the teaching of God who came to bestow blessing on the world, they have replaced it by their own blasphemous creed, and by that substitution have deprived and still deprive milliards of people of the blessing Christ brought to men, and instead of the peace and love he brought have introduced into the world sects, condemnations, murders, and all manner of crimes.

For such readers there are only two ways out: humble confession and renunciation of their lies, or a persecution of those who expose them for what they have done and are still doing.

If they will not disavow their lies, only one thing remains for them: to persecute me - for which I, completing what I have written, prepare myself with joy and with fear of my own weakness.

Leo Tolstoy.
Yasnaya Polyana, 1883.

I: THE SON OF GOD

Man, the son of God, is weak in the flesh but
free in the spirit.

'OUR FATHER'

Mt, i,
18, 19, 24
& 25
The birth of Jesus Christ was thus:

His mother Mary was engaged to Joseph. But before they began to live as man and wife it appeared that Mary was pregnant. Joseph however was a good man and did not wish to shame her: he took her as his wife and had no relations with her till she had given birth to her first son and had named him Jesus.

Lk ii
40 - 52
And the boy grew and matured and was intelligent beyond his years.

When Jesus was twelve years old Mary went once with Joseph for the holiday at Jerusalem and took the boy with her. When the holiday was over they started homeward and forgot about the boy. Then they remembered, but thought he had gone with other lads, and on the way they inquired about him but he was nowhere to be found, so they went back for him to Jerusalem. And not till the third day did they find the boy in the church, where he was sitting with the teachers and asking questions. And everyone was surprised at his intelligence. His mother saw him and said: 'What have you done to us? Your father and I have been looking for you and grieving.' And he said to them: 'But where did you look for me? Surely you knew that a son should be looked for in his Father's house?' And they did not understand him, nor did they understand whom he called his Father.

And after this Jesus lived with his mother and obeyed her in everything. And he advanced in stature and in intelligence. And
Lk iii 23
everyone thought that Jesus was the son of Joseph. And so he lived to the age of thirty.

Mt. iii 1
Mk i   4
At that time a prophet John announced himself in Judea. He lived in the open country of Judea near the Jordan. His dress was of camelhair
Mt iii   4
belted with a strap, and he fed on bark and on herbs.

John said: Bethink yourselves, for the Kingdom of Heaven is at hand.

Mk i   4
He called on the people to change their lives and get rid of wickedness, and as a sign of that change of life he bathed them in the
Lk iii
4 - 6
Jordan. He said: "A voice calls to you; Open a way for God through the

wilderness, level a path for him. Make it so that all may be level, that there may be neither hollows nor hills, neither high nor low. Then God will be among you and all will find salvation."

Lk iii
10 - 14

And the people asked him: What must we do? He replied: Let him that has two suits of clothes give one to him that has none, and let him that has food give to him that has none. And tax-gatherers came to him and asked: What are we to do? He said to them: Extort nothing beyond what is due. And soldiers asked: How are we to live? He said: Do no one any harm, nor defraud any man, and be content with what is served out to you.

And inhabitants of Jerusalem came to him, and the Jews in the neighborhood of Judea near the Jordan. And they acknowledged their wrong-doings to him, and as a sign of a changed life he bathed them in the Jordan.

Mt iii
5 - [9] - 13

And many of the Orthodox and conventional religionists came to John, but secretly. He recognized them and said: You are a race of vipers: or have you also seen that you cannot escape the will of God? Then bethink yourselves and change your faith! And if you wish to change your faith let it be seen by your fruits that you have bethought yourselves. The axe is already laid to the tree. If the tree produces bad fruit it will be cut down and cast into the fire.

As a sign of a changed life I cleanse you in water, but as well as that bathing you must also be cleansed with the spirit. The spirit will cleanse you as a master cleanses his threshing-floor when he gathers the wheat and burns the chaff.

Jesus, too, came from Galilee to the Jordan to be bathed by John, and was bathed and heard John's preaching.

And from the Jordan he went into the wild places and there felt the power of the spirit.

Mt iv
1 - 2

Jesus remained in the desert forty days and forty nights without food or drink.

And the voice of the flesh said to him: If you were the son of Almighty God you could make bread out of stones, but you cannot do so, therefore you are not a son of God.

Lk iv
3 - 4

But Jesus said to himself. If I cannot make bread out of stones, it means that I am not a son of God in the flesh but in the spirit. I am alive not by bread but by the spirit. And my spirit is able to disregard the flesh.

But still hunger tormented him, and the voice of the flesh again said to him: If you live only by the spirit and can disregard the flesh, you can throw off the flesh and your spirit will remain alive.

Lk iv
9 - 12
And it seemed to him that he was standing on the roof of the temple and the voice of the flesh said to him: If you are a son of God in the spirit, throw yourself from the temple, you will not hurt yourself but an unseen force will keep you, support you, and save you from all harm. But Jesus said to himself. I can disregard the flesh, but I may not throw it off, for I was born by the spirit into the flesh. That was the will of the Father of my spirit, and I cannot oppose him.

Then the voice of the flesh said to him: If you cannot oppose your Father by throwing yourself from the temple and discarding life, then you cannot oppose your Father by hungering when you need to eat. You

Lk iv
5 - 8
must not make light of the desires of the flesh; they are placed in you, and you must serve them. Then Jesus seemed to see all the kingdoms of the earth and all the peoples, just as they live and labor for the flesh, expecting gain therefrom. And the voice of the flesh said to him: There, you see, these people work for me and I give them what they wish for. If you will work for me you will have the same. But Jesus said to himself: My Father is not flesh but spirit. I live by him. I am always aware of his presence in me. Him alone I honor and for him alone I work, expecting reward from him alone.

Lk iv
13 - 14
Jn i
35 - 49
Then the temptations ceased and Jesus knew the power of the spirit.

And when he had experienced the power of the spirit, Jesus went out of the wild places and came again to John and stayed with him.

And when Jesus was leaving John, John said of him: That is the saviour of men.

On hearing those words of John two of his pupils left their former teacher and went after Jesus. He, seeing them following him, stopped and said: What do you want? They replied: Teacher, we wish to be with you and to know your teaching. He said: Come with me and I will tell you everything. They went with him and stayed with him, listening to him till ten o'clock.

One of these pupils was called Andrew. He had a brother Simon. Having heard Jesus, Andrew went to his brother Simon and said to him: We have found him of whom the prophets wrote - the Messiah has told us of our salvation. Andrew took Simon and brought him also to Jesus. Jesus called this brother of Andrew's, Peter, which means a stone. And both these brothers became pupils of Jesus.

Afterwards, before entering Galilee, Jesus met Philip and called him to go with him. Philip was from Bethsaida and a fellow-villager of Peter and Andrew. When Philip had got to know Jesus he went and found his brother Nathanael and said to him: We have found the chosen of God of whom Moses and the prophets wrote. This is Jesus, the son of Joseph of Nazareth. Nathanael was surprised that he of whom the prophets wrote should be from a neighboring village, and he said: It is most unlikely that the messenger of God should be from Nazareth. Philip said: Come with me, you shall see and hear for yourself. Nathaniel agreed and went with his brother and met Jesus, and when he had heard him he said to Jesus: Yes, now I see that it is true that you are a son of God and the King of Israel. Jesus said to him: Learn something more important than that: henceforth the heavens are opened and men may be in communion with the heavenly powers. Henceforth God will no longer be separate from men.

Jn i 51

And Jesus came home to Nazareth and on a holiday went as usual into the Assembly and began to read. They gave him the book of the prophet Isaiah; and unrolling it he read. In the book was written: The spirit of the Lord is in me. He has chosen me to announce happiness to the unfortunate and the brokenhearted, to announce freedom to those who are bound, light to the blind, and salvation and rest to the tormented, to announce to all men the day of God's mercy.

Lk iv
16 - 21

He folded the book, returned it to the attendant, and sat down. And all waited to hear what he would say. And he said to them: That writing has now been fulfilled before your eyes.

II: THE SERVICE OF GOD

Therefore man should work not for the flesh,
but for the spirit.

"WHICH ART IN HEAVEN"

Mt xii 1
Mk ii 23
Lk vi 1
It happened that Jesus was walking across a field with his pupils one Saturday. The pupils were hungry, and on the way they plucked ears of corn and rubbed them in their hands and ate the grain. But according to the teaching of the Orthodox, God had given Moses a law that everyone should observe Saturday and do nothing that day. According to the teaching of the Orthodox, God had ordered that anyone who worked on Saturday should be stoned.

Mt xii 2
The Orthodox noticed that the pupils rubbed ears of corn on a Saturday and said to them: It is wrong to do that on a Saturday. One must not work on Saturday, and you are rubbing ears of corn. God made Saturday holy, and commanded that the breaking of it should be punished by death.

Mt xii
7 - 8
Jesus heard this, and said: If you understood what is meant by the words of God: 'I desire love and not sacrifice' - you would not condemn what is harmless. Man is more important than Saturday.

Lk xiii
10 - 14
It happened another time on a Saturday that when Jesus was teaching in the Assembly a sick woman came to him and asked him to help her. And Jesus began to cure her.

Lk xiv 3
The Orthodox church-elder was angry with Jesus, and said to the people: In the law of God it is said: 'There are six days in the week on which to work. But Jesus then asked the Orthodox professors of the law: Do you think it is wrong to help a man on Saturday? And they did not know what to answer.

Lk xiv
6 - 5
Lk xiii 15
Then Jesus said: Deceivers! Does not each of you untie his ox from its manger and take it to water on Saturday? And if his sheep fell into a well would not any one of you pull it out even on Saturday? A man is much better than a sheep: yet you say that it is wrong to help a man. What then do you think we should do on Saturday - good or evil? Save life or destroy it? Good should be done always, even on Saturday.

Mt xii
11 - 12

Mk iii 4

Mt ix 9
Jesus one day saw a tax-gatherer receiving taxes. The tax-gatherer's name was Matthew. Jesus talked to him and Matthew understood him, liked his teaching, and invited him to his house and showed him hospitality.

When Jesus came to Matthew's house some of Matthew's friends were also there tax-gatherers and unbelievers. Jesus did not disdain them, but he and his pupils sat down with them. And when the Orthodox saw him, they said to his pupils: How is it that your teacher eats with tax-gatherers and unbelievers? For according to the teaching of the Orthodox, God forbids any intercourse with unbelievers. Mt ix 10 - 13

Jesus heard this, and said: He who boasts of good health needs no doctor, but a sick man does. Understand what the words of God mean: 'I desire love and not sacrifice.' I cannot teach a change of faith to those who consider themselves Orthodox, but to those who consider themselves unbelievers.

Some Orthodox professors of the law came to Jesus from Jerusalem. And they saw that his pupils, and Jesus himself, ate bread without having washed their hands, and these Orthodox began to blame him for that, for they themselves strictly observed the Church tradition as to how the dishes should be washed, and would not eat unless they had been so washed. And they would also not eat anything from the market until they had washed their hands. Mt xv 1 Mk vii 1 Mt xv 2 Mk vii 2 - 5

And the Orthodox professors of the law asked him: Why do you not follow the Church traditions, but take bread with unwashed hands and eat it? And he answered them: How is it that you with your Church traditions break God's commandment? God said to you: 'Honour your father and mother'. But you have arranged that anyone may say- 'I give to God what I used to give to my parents', and then he is not bound to feed his father and mother. So by the Church tradition you break the law of God. Deceivers! Well did the prophet Isaiah say of you: 'Because these people fall down before me only in words, and honour me only with their tongue, while their heart is far from me; and because their fear of me is only a human law which they have learnt by rote, I will do a wonderful, an extraordinary thing among them: the wisdom of their wise men shall be lost, and the understanding of their thinkers shall be dimmed. Woe to those who seek to hide their desires from the Highest, and who do their deeds in darkness.' Mt xv 3 Mk vii 10 - 13 Mt xv 7 - 9

So it is with you: You neglect what is important in the law - the commandment of God - but observe your own traditions as to the washing of cups. Mk vii 8

And Jesus called the people to him and said: Hear all of you and understand: there is nothing in the world that entering a man can defile him; but what goes forth from him, that can defile a man. Let love and mercy be in your soul, then all will be clean. Try to understand this. Mk vii 14 - 21

And when he returned home his pupils asked him what those words meant. And he said: Do you also not understand? Do you not understand that what is external, bodily, cannot defile a man? For it does not enter his soul but his belly. It enters his belly and passes out again. Only that which goes out of him from his soul can defile a man. For out of a man's soul proceed evil, adulteries, obscenity, murders, thefts, covetousness, wrath, deceit, insolence, envy, calumny, pride, and every kind of folly.

Mk vii 23 And this evil is out of man's soul and it alone can defile him.

Jn ii

13 - 16 After this came the Passover, and Jesus went to Jerusalem and entered the temple. In the courts of the temple were cattle: cows, bulls, and sheep; and there were cotes for pigeons; and money-changers behind their counters. All this was wanted for offerings to God. The animals were killed and offered up in the Temple. That was how the Jews prayed, as they had been taught by the Orthodox professors of the law. Jesus went into the Temple, plaited a whip, drove all the cattle out of the porch, turned out all the doves, and scattered all the money, and bade them not bring such things into the Temple.

Mt xxi 13

Mk xi 17

(Isa lvi 7)

(Jer. vii 4,

11) He said: The prophet Isaiah said to you: 'The house of God is not the Temple in Jerusalem, but the whole world of God's people.' And the prophet Jeremiah also told you: 'Do not believe the falsehood that the house of God is here; do not believe this, but change your lives: do not judge falsely, do not oppress a stranger, a widow, or an orphan, do not shed innocent blood, and do not come into the house of God and say: Now we can quietly do evil. Do not make my house a den of thieves.'

Mk xi

18 - 20 And the Jews objected and said: You say that our way of serving God is wrong. How can you prove that? And Jesus turned to them and said: Destroy this temple and in three days I will raise a new, living temple. And the Jews said: How can you suddenly build a new temple, when Mt xii

6 - 7 this one took forty years to build? And Jesus said to them: I speak to you of what is more important than the temple. You would not speak as you do if you understood the meaning of the prophet's words: 'I, God, do not rejoice in your sacrifices, but in your love of one another.' The living temple is the whole world of men when they love one another.

Jn ii

23 - 25 And many people in Jerusalem believed in what he said. But he himself believed in nothing external for he knew that everything is within man. He had no need that anyone should give witness of man, for he knew that the spirit is in man.

Jn iv

4 - 10 And Jesus had once to pass through Samaria. He came to the Samaritan village of Sychar, near the place that Jacob gave to his son Joseph. Jacob's well was there, and Jesus, being tired by his journey, sat

down by it while his pupils went into the town to fetch bread.

And a woman came from Sychar to draw water, and Jesus asked her to give him to drink. She said to him: How is it that you ask me to give you water? For you Jews have no dealings with us Samaritans.

But he said to her: If you knew me and knew what I teach you would not say that, but would give me to drink and I would give you the water of life. Whoever drinks of the water from this well will thirst again, but whoever drinks of the water of life shall always be satisfied, and it will bring him to everlasting life. Jn iv 13 - 14

The woman understood that he was speaking of divine things, and said to him: I see that you are a prophet and wish to teach me. But how can you teach me divine things when you are a Jew and I am a Samaritan? Our people pray to God upon this mountain, but you Jews say that the house of God is only in Jerusalem. You cannot teach me divine things, for you have one religion and we have another. Jn iv 19 - 21

Then Jesus said to her: Believe me, woman, the time has arrived when people will come neither to this mountain nor to Jerusalem to pray to the Father. The time has come when the real worshippers of God will honour the heavenly Father in spirit and by their works. The Father has need of such worshippers. The woman did not understand what he meant by saying that God is a spirit, and she said: I have heard that a messenger of God will come, he whom they call the anointed. He will tell us everything. Jn iv 23 - 26

Jesus said to her: It is I who am speaking to you. Do not expect anything more.

After this Jesus came to the country of the Jews and lived there with his pupils and taught. At that time John was teaching near Salim, and bathing people in the river Enon, for he had not yet been imprisoned. Jn iii 22 - 27

And a dispute arose between John's pupils and those of Jesus as to which was better - John's cleansing by water, or the teaching of Jesus. And they came to John and said to him: You cleanse with water, but Jesus only teaches, and all go to him. What do you say about him?

John said: A man can of himself teach nothing unless God teach him. He who speaks of the earth is of the earth, but he who speaks of God is from God. It cannot be proved whether spoken words are from God or not from God. God is a spirit; He cannot be measured and cannot be proved. He who understands the words of the spirit proves thereby that he is of the spirit. The Father, loving his son, has entrusted everything to him. He who believes in the son has life, but he who does not believe in the son has no life. God is the spirit in man. Jn iii 31 - 36

Lk xi
37 - 41

After this one of the Orthodox came to Jesus and invited him to dinner. Jesus went in and sat down to table. The Orthodox man noticed that Jesus did not wash before the meal and was surprised. Jesus said to him: You Orthodox people wash everything outside, but is everything clean within you? Be kind to all men and everything will be clean.

Lk vii
37 - 50

And while he was in the house of the Orthodox man, a woman of the town, who was a wrong-doer came there. She had learnt that Jesus was in that house and came there and brought a bottle of perfume. And she knelt at his feet and wept, and wetting his feet with her tears wiped them with her hair, and poured the perfume over them.

The Orthodox man saw this and thought to himself: He can hardly be a prophet. If he were really a prophet he would know what sort of a woman it is that is washing his feet: he would know that she is a wrong-doer and would not let her touch him.

Jesus, guessing his thought, turned to him and said: Shall I tell you what I think? Yes, do so, replied his host. Then Jesus said: There were two men who held themselves debtors to one master, one for five hundred pieces of money and the other for fifty. And neither of them had anything to pay with. And the creditor forgave them both. Which of them do you think would love the creditor and care for him most? The host replied: He of course that owed most.

Then Jesus pointed to the woman and said: So it is with you and this woman. You consider yourself Orthodox. And therefore a small debtor; she considers herself wrong-doer and therefore a great debtor. I came into your house and you did not give me water to wash my feet; she washes them with her tears and wipes them with her hair. You did not kiss me, but she kisses my feet. You gave me no oil for my head, but she anoints my feet with precious perfume. He who considers himself Orthodox will not do works of love; only he who considers himself a wrong-doer will do them. And for works of love everything is forgiven. And he said to her: Your wickedness is forgiven you. And Jesus said:. Everything depends on what a man considers himself to be. He who considers himself good will not be good, but he who considers himself bad is good.

Lk xviii
10 - 14

And he added: Two men came into the Temple to pray. One was Orthodox, and the other was a tax-farmer.

The Orthodox man prayed: I thank thee, God, that I am not as other men, not miserly, nor a libertine, nor a deceiver, nor such a wretch as that tax-farmer. I fast twice a week, and give away a tenth of my property.

But the tax-farmer stood far away, and dared not look up to heaven but only beat his breast, saying: God, look upon me, sinner that I am.

This was a better prayer than that of the Orthodox man, for he who exalts himself abases himself, and he who humbles himself raises himself.

Then some pupils of John came to Jesus and said: Why do your pupils not fast, while we and the Orthodox fast a great deal? The law of God orders fasting. Lk v 33 - 38

And Jesus said to them: While the bridegroom is at the wedding no one grieves. Only when the bridegroom has gone do they grieve.

Having life, one should not grieve. The external service of God cannot be combined with the activity of love. The old teaching of external service of God cannot be combined with my teaching of active love of one's neighbour. To unite my teaching with the old is like tearing a piece from a new garment and sewing it onto an old one. The new one will be torn and the old one will not be mended. Either all my teaching must be accepted or all the old, and having accepted my teaching it is impossible to keep the old teaching of purification, fasting, and keeping Saturday - just as new wine must not be poured into old wine-skins, or the old skins will burst and the wine will be spilt. New wine must be put into new wineskins and then they will both be preserved.

III: THE SOURCE OF LIFE

*The life of all men proceeds from
the spirit of the Father.*

'HALLOWED BE THY NAME'

Mt xi
2 - 7

Later on, some of John's pupils came to ask Jesus whether it was he of whom John spoke: Did he reveal the Kingdom of God and renew men by the spirit?

Jesus answered and said: Look for yourselves, and listen to the teaching - and tell John whether the Kingdom of God has begun and whether people are being renewed by the spirit. Tell him what Kingdom of God I am preaching. It is said in the prophecies that when the Kingdom of God comes all men will be blessed. Tell him that my Kingdom of God is such that the poor are blessed, and so is everyone who understands the teaching.

And having let John's pupils go, Jesus began to speak to the people about the Kingdom of God that John announced. He said: When you went to John in the wilderness to be baptized, what did you go to see? Orthodox teachers of the law went to see John too, but they did Mt xi 16 not understand what he was talking about, and considered him of no account. Those Orthodox teachers of the law only consider true what they themselves invent and hear from one another, or the law they Mt xi 18 - 19 have themselves devised; but what John says and what I say, they do not listen to and do not understand. Of what John says they have only understood that he fasts in the wilderness, and they say: 'There is a devil in him. Of what I say they have understood only that I do not fast, and they say: 'He eats and drinks with tax-gatherers and sinners - he is Mt xi 17 a friend of theirs.' They are like children in the street who chatter to one another and wonder that no one listens to them. And you may judge of Mt xi 8 - 10 their wisdom by what they do. If you went to John to see a man dressed in rich clothes - why, such men live here in the palaces. What then is it you went to see in the wilderness? Did you go because you think John is like other prophets? Do not think so! John is not a prophet like the others. He is more than all the prophets. The others foretold what might happen. He announces what is: namely, that the Kingdom of God was, and is, here on earth. I tell you truly: no one greater than John has ever been born. He has declared the Kingdom of God on earth and is therefore above all the others. The law and the prophets were necessary Lk xvi 16 till John came, but now he has announced that the Kingdom of God is on earth, and that he who makes an effort can enter into it.

And some of the Orthodox came to Jesus and asked him: How Lk xvii 20 and when will the Kingdom of God come? And he answered them: The Kingdom of God which I preach is not what the former prophets preached. They said that God would come with diverse visible signs, but I speak of a Kingdom of God the coming of which cannot be seen with the eyes. And if anyone tells you: See, it has come, or is coming; Lk xvii 23 - 24 or, See, it is here, or there; do not believe them. The Kingdom of God is not in any definite time or place. It is like lightning - here, there and everywhere. And it has neither time nor place, for the Kingdom of God Lk xvii 21 that I preach is within you.

After that, one of the Orthodox, a Jewish ruler named Nicodemus, Jn iii 1 - 21 came to Jesus at night and said: You do not bid men keep Saturday, or tell them to observe cleanliness, or to offer sacrifices, or to fast, and you would abolish the temple, and say that God is a spirit and that the Kingdom of God is within us. What is this Kingdom of God?

And Jesus answered him: Understand that if man is conceived from heaven there must be something heavenly in him. You must be born again.

Nicodemus did not understand this, and said: How can a man, born of the flesh and grown up, return to his mother's womb and be conceived afresh?

And Jesus answered him: Understand what I say: I say that man is born not from the flesh alone but also from the spirit, and so every man is conceived of flesh and of spirit, and therefore the kingdom of heaven is within him. Of the flesh he is flesh, From flesh spirit cannot be born; spirit can come only from spirit. The spirit is the living thing within you which lives in freedom and reason; it is that of which you know neither the beginning nor the end and which every man feels within him. So why do you wonder that I said that we must be born from heaven?

Nicodemus said: Still I do not believe that this can be so.

Then Jesus said to him: What kind of a teacher are you if you do not understand this? Understand that I am not talking any kind of mystery; I speak of what we all know, and assure you of what we all see. How will you believe in what is in heaven if you do not believe in what is on earth and within yourself?

No one has ever gone up to heaven, and we have only man on earth who has come from heaven and is himself of heaven. It is this heavenly son of man that must be exalted, that all may believe in him and not perish but have heavenly life. Not for man's destruction, but for their good, did God implant in man this son of his, like unto Himself. He gave him that everyone should believe in him and not perish but have eternal life. He did not bring this son of his (this inner life) into the world of men to destroy it, but brought forth his son (this inner life) that the world of men should live by him.

He who commits his life to this son of man does not die, but he who does not commit his life to him destroys himself by not trusting to what is life itself.

Division (death) consists in this, that life came into the world, but men go away from that life.

Light is the life of men; light came into the world, but men prefer darkness to light, and do not go to the light. He who does wrong avoids the light that his deeds may not be seen, and so deprives himself of life. But he who lives in the truth goes to the light that his deeds may be seen, and he has life and is united to God.

The Kingdom of God must be understood not as you imagine - that the Kingdom of God will come for all men at a certain time and in a certain place - but thus: in the whole world there are always some people who rely on the heavenly son of man, and these become sons of the Kingdom; the others who do not rely on him perish. The Father of the spirit in man is the Father of those only who acknowledge themselves as his sons. And therefore only those exist to him who have preserved within them what he gave them.

Mt xiii
3 - 5

After this Jesus began to explain to the people what the Kingdom of God is, and he taught it them by parables.

He said: The Father - who is the spirit - sows the life of understanding in the world as a husbandman sows grain in his field. He sows over the whole field without remarking which seeds fall in what place. And some seeds fall on the path and the birds come and eat it. Other seeds fall among stones and though they come up they wither, because there

Mt xiii
7 - 8

is no room for their roots. Others again fall among wormwood and the wormwood chokes them, and though ears form they do not fill. But other seeds fall on good ground and grow and make up for the lost seed, and bear ears which fill, and which yield thirtyfold, or sixtyfold, or a hundredfold. So God also has sown the spirit broadcast in man: in some it is lost but in others it yields a hundredfold. It is these last that form the Kingdom of God.

Mk iv 26-29

So the Kingdom of God is not what you imagine - that God will come to reign over you. God has sown the spirit, and the Kingdom of God will be only in those who preserve it.

God does not force men but, like a sower, casts seed on the ground and thinks no more of it. The seed itself swells, sprouts, puts forth leaf, stalk, and ears that fill with grain. Only when it has ripened does the husbandman send reapers to gather in the harvest. In the same way God gave His Son - the spirit - to the world; and the spirit grows in the world of itself, and the sons of the spirit make up the Kingdom of God.

A woman puts yeast into a kneading trough and mixes it with flour. Mt xiii 33 She then mixes it no more but lets the yeast and the bread rise. As long as people live God does not interfere with their life. He gave the spirit to the world and the spirit lives in men, and those who live by the spirit constitute the Kingdom of God. For the spirit there is neither death nor evil. Death and evil exist for the flesh but not for the spirit.

The Kingdom of God may be compared to this: a farmer sowed Mt xiii 24 - 25 good seed in his field. The farmer is the spirit, the Father; the field is the world; the good seed are the sons of the Kingdom of God. Then the farmer lay down to sleep and an enemy came and sowed darnel in the field. The enemy is temptation, and the darnel represents those who yield to temptation. Then the laborers came to the farmer and said: Can Mt xiii 27 - 30 you have sown bad seed? Much darnel has come up on your field. Send us to weed it out. And the farmer said: No, do not do that, or in weeding out the darnel you will trample the wheat. Let them grow together. When the harvest comes I will tell the reapers to gather the darnel and burn it, but the wheat I will store in the barn. The harvest is the end of human life, the harvesters are the powers of heaven. They will burn the darnel, but the wheat will be winnowed and gathered. So also at life's end all that was temporary illusion will perish, and the true life of the spirit will alone be left. Evil does not exist for the Father, the spirit. The spirit keeps what it needs and what is not of it does not exist for it.

The kingdom of heaven is like a net. When spread out in the sea it Mt xiii 47 - 48 catches all kinds of fish, and when it is drawn in, the worthless fish are set aside and thrown back into the sea. So will it be at the end of the age: the powers of heaven will take the good and the evil will be cast away.

And when he had finished speaking, his pupils asked him what these Mt xiii 10 - 11 parables meant. And he said to them: These parables must be understood in two ways. I speak all these parables because there are some like you, my pupils, who understand what the Kingdom of God consists of, and understand that it is within each man, and understand how to enter it;

Mt xiii
14 - 15 but others do not understand this. They look but do not see, they hear but do not understand, for their hearts have become gross. So I speak these parables with two meanings, for these people and for those. To the others I speak of God, of what His Kingdom is for Him, and they may understand that. But for you I speak of what the Kingdom of God is for you - the kingdom that is within you.

Mt xiii
18 - 23 And see that you understand the parable of the sower rightly. For you that parable means this: To everyone who has understood the meaning Of the Kingdom of God, but has not accepted it in his heart, evil comes and robs him of what was sown; this is the seed by the wayside. That which was sown on stony ground represents the man who receives the teaching readily and gladly, but has no root and only accepts it for a time, and as soon as pressure and persecution comes because of the meaning of the kingdom, he at once denies it. That which is sown among the wormwood is he who understands the meaning of the kingdom, but worldly cares and eagerness for riches strangle the meaning in him and he does not bear fruit. And that which was sown on good ground is he who understands the meaning of the kingdom and takes it into his heart; he bears fruit a hundredfold, or sixtyfold, or Mt xiii 12 thirtyfold. For to him that keeps the spirit much is given; but from him who does not keep it everything will be taken away.

Lk viii 18 So see how you understand these parables. Understand them so as not to yield to deceptions, wrong-doings, and cares, but so as to yield thirtyfold, sixtyfold, or a hundredfold.

Mt viii 31 The kingdom of heaven in the soul grows up from nothing but gives everything. It is like a birch-seed, which is a very small seed, but when it grows up becomes a very big tree, and the birds of heaven build their nests in it.

IV: THE KINGDOM OF GOD

*Therefore the will of the Father is the life and
we are of all men.*

"THY KINGDOM COME"

Jesus went about in the towns and villages and taught all men the happiness of doing the Father's will. And he was sorry for people because they perish without knowing what true life consists of, and trouble and torment themselves without knowing why, like scattered sheep that have no shepherd. `Mt ix 35 - 36`

Once many people came to Jesus to hear his teaching and he went up on a hill and sat down. His pupils surrounded him. And he began to teach the people what the Father's will is. He said: `Mt v 1 - 2`

Blessed are the poor and the homeless, for they live in the will of the Father. If they are hungry they shall be satisfied, and if they sorrow and weep they shall be comforted. If people despise them, thrust them aside, and drive them away, let them be glad of it, for so God's people have always been treated and they receive a heavenly reward. `Lk vi 20 - 26`

But woe to the rich, for they have already got what they wanted, and will get nothing more. Now they are satisfied, but they too will be hungry. Now they rejoice, but they too will be sad. Woe to those whom everyone praises, for only deceivers are praised by everybody.

Blessed are the poor and homeless; but blessed only if they are poor not merely outwardly but also in spirit - just as salt is good only when it has saltness in it and is not salt merely in appearance.

So you also, the poor and homeless, are the teachers of the world; you are blessed if you know that true happiness is in being homeless and poor. But if you are poor only outwardly then, like salt that has no savor, you are good for nothing. You are the light of the world, therefore do not hide your light but let men see it. When a man lights a candle he does not put it under the bench but on the table that it should give light to everyone in the room. So you, too, should not hide your light but show it by your actions, that men may see that you have the truth, and seeing your good deeds may understand your heavenly Father. `Mt v 13 - 24`

And do not think that I free you from the law. I teach not release from the law but fulfillment of the eternal law. As long as there are men under heaven the eternal law remains. There will be no release from law till men of themselves fulfill the eternal law completely. And now, I give you the commandments of that eternal law. If anyone releases himself from any of these short commandments and teaches others that they may do so, he shall be least in the kingdom of heaven, but he who fulfills them and thereby teaches others to fulfill them shall be great in the kingdom of heaven. For if your virtue is no more than the virtue of the Orthodox legalists you will never reach the kingdom of heaven.

These are the commandments:

I

In the former law it was said: Do not kill, and if anyone kills another he must be judged.

But I tell you that everyone who grows angry with his brother-man deserves judgment, and still more to blame is he who speaks abusively to his brother-man.

So if you wish to pray to God, first think whether there is anyone who has something against you. If you remember even one man who considers that you have offended him, leave your prayers and go first to make peace with your brother-man, and then you may pray. Know that God requires neither sacrifice nor prayer, but only peace, concord, and love among men; and that you can neither pray nor think of God if there is a single man towards whom you do not feel love.

So this is the first commandment: Do not be angry, and do not rail; and if you have spoken harshly to anyone make peace with him and do it so that no one should have a grudge against you.

II

Mt v 31

In the former law it was said: Do not commit adultery, and if you wish to put away your wife, give her a letter of divorcement.

Mt v
28 - 29

But I tell you that if you look lustfully at a woman's beauty you are already committing adultery. All sensuality destroys the soul, and so it is better for you to renounce the pleasures of the flesh than to destroy your life.

Mt v 32

And if you put away your wife, then besides being vicious yourself you drive her to wantonness too, as well as him with whom she may unite.

So that is the second commandment: Do not think that love of a woman is good, do not desire women, but live with her with whom you have become united, and do not leave her.

III

In the former law it was said: Do not utter the name of the Lord God in vain, do not call upon God when lying, and do not dishonor the name of your God. Do not swear to any untruth and so profane your God. Mt v 33 - 41

But I tell you that every oath is a profanation of God. Therefore do not swear at all. Man cannot promise anything, for he is wholly in the power of the Father. He cannot make one gray hair black. How then can he swear beforehand that he will do this or that, and swear to it by God? Every oath is a profanation of God, for if a man is compelled to fulfill under an oath that which is against the will of God it shows that he had promised to act contrary to God's will, and so every oath is an evil. But when men ask you about anything, say Yes if it is yes, or no if it is no; anything added to that is evil.

So the third commandment is: Never swear anything for anyone. Say Yes when it is yes, No when it is no, and understand that every oath is evil.

IV

In the former law it was said that if a man killed another he must give a life for a life, an eye for an eye, a tooth for a tooth, an arm for an arm, an ox for an ox, a slave for a slave, and much else. Mt v 43

But I say to you: Do not fight evil by evil, and not only do not exact at law an ox for an ox, a slave for a slave, a life for a life, but do not resist evil at all. If anyone wishes to take an ox from you, give him another; if he wants to take your coat by law, give him your shirt as well; if anyone knocks out a tooth on one side, turn the other side to him. If he would make you do one piece of work for him, do two. If men wish to take your property, let them have it. If they owe you money and do not return it, do not demand it. Mt vi 30

And therefore: Do not judge or go to law, do not punish, and you yourself will not be judged or punished. Forgive everyone and you will be forgiven; but if you judge others they will judge you also. Mt vi 37

You cannot judge, for men are all blind and do not see the truth. How can you see a speck in your brother's eye when there is dust in your own? You must first get your own eye clear - but whose eyes are perfectly clear? Can a blind man lead the blind? They will both fall into the pit. And those who judge and punish are like blind men leading the blind. Mt vii 1 Mt vii 3 Lk vi 39 - 40

Those who judge, and condemn others to violent treatment, wounds, mutilation, or death, wish to correct them, but what can come of their teaching except that the pupils will learn to become just like their teacher? What then will they do when they have learnt the lesson? Only what their teacher does: violence and murder.

Mt vi 6 And do not expect to find justice in the courts. To entrust one's love of justice to men's courts is like throwing precious pearls to swine: they will trample on them and will tear you to pieces.

And therefore the fourth commandment is: However men may wrong you, do not return evil, do not judge or go to law, do not sue, and do not punish.

V

Mt vi
43 - 44 In the former law it was said: Do good to men of your own nation and do harm to foreigners.

But I tell you: Love not only your own countrymen, but people of other nations also. Let others hate you, attack you, and wrong you, Mt vi 46 but speak well of them and do good to them. If you are attached only to your own countrymen, remember that all men are attached to their Mt vi 45 own countrymen, and wars result from that. But behave equally well to men of all nations, and you will be sons of the Father. All men are His children, so they are all brothers to you.

And so this is the fifth commandment: Treat foreigners as I have told you to treat one another. To the Father of all men there are no separate nations or separate kingdoms: all are brothers, all sons of one Father. Make no distinctions among people as to nations and kingdoms.

And so:
1. Do not be angry, but live at peace with all men.
2. Do not indulge yourself in sexual gratification.
3. Do not promise anything on oath to anyone.
4. Do not resist evil, do not judge and do not go to law.
5. Make no distinction of nationality, but love foreigners as your own people.

Mt vii 12 All these commandments are contained in one:

All that you wish men to do to you, do you to them.

Mt vi
1 - 13 Do not fulfill these commandments for praise from men. If you do it for men, then from men you have your reward. But if you do it not for men, your reward is from your heavenly Father. So if you do good to others do not boast about it before men. That is what the hypocrites do, to obtain praise. And they get what they seek. But if you do good to men, do it so that no one sees it, and that your left hand should not

know what your right hand does. And your Father will see it and will give you what you need.

And if you wish to pray, do not do it as the hypocrites do. They love to pray in the churches and in the sight of men. They do it for men's praise, and from men receive what they aim at.

But if you wish to pray, go where no one will see you, and pray to the Father of your spirit, and He will see what is in your soul and will give you what your soul desires.

When you pray, do not wag your tongue as the hypocrites do. Your Father knows what you need before you open your lips.

Pray only thus:

> *Our Father, without beginning and without end, like the heavens!*
>
> *May Thy being alone be holy.*
>
> *May power be Thine alone, so that Thy will may be done, without beginning and without end, on earth.*
>
> *Give me the food of life this present day.*
>
> *Efface my former mistakes and wipe them out, as I efface and wipe out all the mistakes my brothers have made; that I may not fall into temptation, but be saved from evil.*
>
> *For the power and strength are Thine, and the decision is Thine.*

If you pray, free yourself above all from malice against anyone. For if you do not forgive others their faults, your Father will not forgive you yours. ^{Mk xi 25 - 26}

If you fast, do so without any parade of it before others. The hypocrites fast that people should see it and praise them - and people do praise them, so they get what they wanted. But you should not do so; if you suffer want, go about with a cheerful face that men may not see, but that your Father may see and give you what you need. ^{Mt vi 16 - 34}

Do not lay up store for yourself on earth. On earth maggots consume, and rust eats, and thieves steal: but lay up for yourselves heavenly riches. Heavenly riches are not consumed by maggots, nor eaten away by rust, nor do thieves steal them. Where your riches are, there will your heart be also.

The light of the body is the eye, and the light of the soul is the heart. If your eye is dim your whole body will be in darkness. And if the light of your heart is dim your whole soul will be in darkness. You cannot serve two masters at the same time. If you please the one you will offend the other. You cannot serve both God and the flesh. Either you will work for the earthly life or for God. Therefore do not be anxious about what you will eat or drink, or how you will be dressed. For the life is more wonderful than food and clothing and God has given you this.

Look on God's creatures, the birds. They do not sow or reap or gather in the harvest, yet God feeds them. In God's sight man is not less than a bird. If God gave man life, He will be able to feed him too. And you yourselves know that you can do nothing of yourselves, however you may strive. You cannot lengthen your life by an hour. And why do you trouble about clothing? The flowers of the field do no work and do not spin, but they are adorned as Solomon in all his luxury never was.

And if God has so adorned the grass which grows to-day, and to-morrow is cut down, will He not clothe you?

Do not be afraid and do not worry; do not say that you must think of what you will eat and how you will be clothed. All men need these things and God knows that you need them. So do not trouble about the future. Live in the present day. Take care to be in the Father's will. Desire that which alone is important, and the rest will come of itself. Seek only to be in the will of the Father, and do not trouble about the future, for when it comes its trouble will come too. There is enough evil in the present.

Lk xi 9
Mt vii
9 - 11

Ask and it shall be given you; seek and ye shall find; knock and it will be opened to you. Where is there a father who would give his son a stone instead of bread, or a snake instead of a fish? Then why do you think if we wicked men can give our children what they need, that your Father in heaven will not give you what you truly need, if you ask Him? Ask, and the heavenly Father will give the spirit of life to them that ask Him.

Mt vii
13 - 14

Narrow is the path to life, but enter by that narrow way. There is only one entry to life - a strait and narrow one. Great and wide is the field around, but it leads to destruction. The narrow way alone leads to

Lk xii 32

life, and few find it. But do not be afraid, little flock! The Father has prepared the Kingdom for you.

Mt vi
15 - 17

Only, beware of false prophets and teachers; they come to you in sheep's clothing, but inwardly are ravening wolves. By their fruits - by what comes from them - you will know them. From the burdock you do not gather grapes, nor apples from an aspen. A good tree bears good fruit and a bad tree bad fruit. So you will know these men by the fruits of their teaching.

A good man out of his good heart brings forth all that is good. But an evil man out of his evil heart brings forth all that is evil. For from the overflow of the heart the lips speak. And therefore if teachers tell you to do to others what would be bad for yourselves, if they teach violence, executions, and wars - then you may know that they are false teachers.

For it is not those who say: 'Lord, Lord!' who will enter the kingdom of heaven, but those who fulfill the will of the heavenly Father. The false teachers will say: 'Lord, Lord! We taught your doctrine, and by your teaching drove out evil. But I will disown them and say: 'No, I never recognized you and do not recognize you now, Go away from me; you do what is unlawful.'

He who hears these words of mine and acts on them is like a reasonable man who builds his house on a rock. And his house will stand against all storms. But he who hears these words of mine and does not act on them is like a foolish man who builds his house on the sand. When a storm comes his house will fall and all in it will perish.

And the people were all astonished at this teaching, for the teaching of Jesus was quite different from that of the Orthodox professors of the law. They taught a law that had to be obeyed, but Jesus taught that all men are free. And in Jesus Christ were fulfilled the prophecies of Isaiah: that a people living in darkness, in the shadow of death, saw the light of life. That he who brought this light of truth did no violence or harm to men, but was meek and gentle. To bring truth into the world he neither disputes nor shouts, nor is his voice raised, and he will not break a straw or put out the smallest light, and all the hope of men is in his teaching.

V: THE TRUE LIFE

*The satisfaction of the personal will leads to death;
the satisfaction of the Father's will gives true life.*

"THY WILL BE DONE"

Mt xi 25 And Jesus rejoiced in the power of the spirit and said:

I acknowledge the spirit of the Father, the source of everything in heaven and earth, who has revealed what was hidden from the wise and learned to the simple, because they acknowledge themselves sons of the Father.

Mt xi
28-38 All who are concerned for the happiness of the body have put on a yoke not made for them, and have harnessed themselves to a load they cannot draw.

Understand my teaching and follow it and you shall have peace and joy in life. I give you another yoke and another load - the spiritual life. Yoke yourselves to this, and you shall learn from me peace and happiness.

Be tranquil and meek-hearted and you will find blessedness in your life. For my teaching is a yoke made for you, and to obey my teaching is to have a light load with a yoke suited to you.

Once when he was asked whether he wished to eat, he replied: I have food you do not know of. They thought someone had brought him food, but he said:

My food is to do the will of Him who gave me life and to accomplish what he has entrusted to me. Do not say: There is still time, as a farmer says while waiting for the harvest. He who fulfills the will of the Father is always satisfied and knows neither hunger nor thirst. The fulfillment of the will of God always satisfies and is always a reward in itself. You must not say: 'I will do the will of God later.' While you have life you always can and should do the will of the Father. Our life is a field God has sown, and our business is to gather its fruits. If we gather its fruits we receive the reward of a life beyond time. We do not give ourselves life, someone else gives it us. And if we labor to gather in life, then like harvestmen, we receive a reward. I teach you to gather in this life which the Father gives you.

Jn v 1, 2, 4 Once Jesus went to Jerusalem. There was then a bathing-place in the city, of which people said that an angel came down into it, and that his coming stirred the water and he who first plunged in after that would be cured of whatever illness he had. There were shelters set up around the pool, and under those shelters sick people lay, waiting for the water in the pool to bubble, in order to plunge into it.

Jn v 2-3

And there was a man who had been there thirty-eight years, and was weak.

Jn v 5 - 11

Jesus asked him what ailed him. And the man told him that he had been ill for thirty-eight years and was waiting to get into the pool first after the water bubbled, in order to be healed, but all these thirty-eight years he had not been able to get in first for someone always got into the pool before him.

And Jesus saw that the man was old, and said to him: Do you wish to get well?

The man replied: Yes, I do wish to, but I have no one to help me into the pool in time. Someone always gets in before me.

And Jesus said to him: Arouse yourself, take up your bedding and go.

And the sick man took up his bedding and walked away.

And it was on a Saturday. And the Orthodox said: You must not carry your bedding for today is Saturday.

He replied: He who raised me told me to take up my bedding.

Jn v 11

And the infirm man went away and told the Orthodox that it was Jesus who had cured him. And they were angry, And accused Jesus because he did such things on Saturday.

Jn v 15 - 17

And Jesus said: What the Father always does, I also do. I tell you truly: the son can do nothing for himself; he does only what he has understood from the Father. What the Father does, he also does. The Father loves the son, and has taught him all the things the son needs to know.

Jn v 19 - 31

As the Father gives life to the dead so the son gives life to him who desires it, because as the business of the Father is life so the business of the son must be life. The Father has not condemned men to death, but has given them power to die or live at will. And if they Honor the son as the Father they will live.

I tell you truly that he who has understood my teaching and believed in the common Father of all men, has life already and is delivered from death. They who have understood the meaning of human life have already escaped from death and will always live. For as the Father has life in Himself so He has given the son to have life in himself also, and has given him freedom. It is in this way that he is the son of man.

Henceforth mortals are divided into two kinds: those who do good and thereby find life, and those who do evil and are thereby destroyed. And this is not my decision, but is what I have understood from the Father. And my decision is just, for I decide so not in order to do what I wish, but in order that all may do the will of the Father of all men.

Jn v
36 - 40

If I assure you that my teaching is true, that does not confirm my teaching; what confirms it is the conduct I teach. That shows that I do not teach from myself but from the Father of all men. And my Father, He who has taught me, confirms the truth of my commandments in the souls of all.

But you do not wish to understand or to know His voice. And you do not accept the meaning that voice declares. You do not wish to believe in that voice in yourselves which is the spirit that has descended from heaven.

Enter into the meaning of your scriptures. You will find in them the same as in my teaching: commands to live not for yourselves alone but to do good to men. Why then do you not wish to believe my commandments - which are those that give life to all men? I teach you in the name of the common Father of all men, and you do not accept my teaching, but if someone teaches you in his own name, him you believe.

Jn v
43 - 44

You should not believe all that people say to one another, but must believe only that there is in every man a son like the Father.

Lk ix
11 - 22

And that men should not think that the kingdom of heaven is something visible - but should understand that it consists in fulfillment of the Father's will and that that fulfillment depends on each man's efforts - and that people might understand that life is given not for oneself personally but only for the fulfillment of the Father's will, which alone saves from death and gives life, Jesus spoke a parable, and said:

There was a rich man who had to leave home. Before he set out he called his slaves and gave them ten pounds, one to each, and said: While I am away, work each of you, at what I have set you. And it happened that when he had gone, some of the people of that town said: We do not wish to serve him any more.

When the rich man returned, he called the slaves to whom he had given the money, and asked what each of them had done with it.

The first one came and said: See, master, with your one pound I have earned ten. And the master said to him: Well done, good slave, you have been faithful in a small matter and I will set you over much: be one with me in all my estate.

A second slave came and said: See master, with your pound I have earned five. And the master said to him: Well done, good slave, be one with me in all my estate.

Another one came and said: See, here is your pound. I put it in a cloth and buried it because I was afraid of you. You are a hard man, you take where you did not store and gather where you did not sow.

And the master said to him: Foolish slave! I will judge you by your own words. You say that from fear of me you hid the pound in the earth and did not make use of it. If you knew that I am severe and take where I have not given, then why did you not do as I bade you? If you had used my pound the estate would have been added to and you would have fulfilled what I bade you. But now you have not done what the pound was given you for, and so you must not have it. Mt xxv 25-26 Lk ix 23 - 26

And the master had the pound taken from him who had not used it and given to him who had done most. But the slaves remonstrated, and said to him: Master, he has a great deal already. But the master said: Give to him who worked much, for to him who looks after what he has, more shall be given. Drive out those who did not wish to be in my power, and let none of them remain. Mt xxv 30

The master is the source of life, the spirit, the Father. His slaves are men. The pounds are the life of the spirit. As the master did not work on his estate himself but told the slaves each to work by himself, so also the spirit of life in men has told them to work for the life of all men, and has then left them alone. Those who sent to say that they did not acknowledge the master's power are those who do not acknowledge the spirit of life. The return of the master and his call for an account is the destruction of the bodily life and the decision of the people's fate: whether they have increased the life that was given them. Some, those slaves who fulfill the master's will, use what is given them and greatly increase it. These are they who, having received life, understand that life is the will of the Father and is given them to serve the life of others. The foolish and wicked slave who hid his pound and did not use it, represents those who only follow their own desires and not the will of the Father, and do not serve the life of others. The slaves who fulfill the Master's will and work to increase his estate become sharers in the master's whole estate, but the slaves who do not fulfill the master's will and do not work for him are bereft of what was given them. Men who fulfill the Father's will and serve life become sharers in the life of the Father and receive more life notwithstanding the destruction of the flesh. Those who do not fulfill the will and do not serve life are bereft of what life they had, and are destroyed. Those who do not wish to acknowledge the master's authority do not exist for him: he drives them forth. Those who do not acknowledge the life of the spirit within themselves - the life of the son of man - do not exist for the Father.

Jn vi
1 - 3
Jn vi 5
Jn vi 7
Mt xiv 17
Jn vi
9 - 11

After this Jesus went into a desert place and many people followed him. He went up a hill and sat down there with his pupils. And he saw many people coming and said: Where can we get bread for all these people? Philip said: Even two hundred pennyworth would not be enough to give each of them something. We have only a little bread and fish. And another pupil said: Some of them have bread: there is a boy who has five loaves and two small fishes. And Jesus said: Tell them all to lie down on the grass.

And Jesus took the bread he had, and gave it to his pupils and bade them give it to the other people. And so they all began to give to one another what they had, and they all had enough to eat and much was left over.

Jn vi
26 - 33

Next day the people again came to Jesus, and he said to them: You come to me not because you have seen wonders, but because you ate bread and were satisfied. Do not work for food which perishes, but for food which will last for ever, such as only the spirit of the son of man, sealed by the Father, gives you.

The Jews said: What must we do to fulfill the will of God?

And Jesus said: The work of God consists in believing in the life He has given you.

They said: Give us proofs that we may believe. What do you do? Our fathers ate manna in the wilderness. God gave them food to eat, so it is written.

Jesus answered them: The true heavenly bread is the spirit of the son of man, which the Father gives. For the food of man is the spirit that descends from heaven. It is that which gives life to the world.

Jn vi
35 - 57

My teaching gives true nourishment. He who follows me will not hunger, and he who believes in my teaching will never know thirst. But I have already told you that you have seen this and yet do not believe.

All that life which the Father has given to the son will be realized by my teaching, and everyone who believes in it will share that life. For I came down from heaven not to do my own will but the will of the Father who gave me life. And the will of the Father who sent me is that I should keep all the life He gave and not lose any of it. So it is the will of the Father who sent me, that everyone who sees the son and believes in him should have everlasting life. And my teaching gives life at the last day (of the flesh).

The Jews were disturbed at his saying that his teaching had come down from heaven. They said: Why, this is Jesus the son of Joseph: we know his father and mother. How is it that he says his teaching has come down from heaven?

And Jesus said: Do not discuss who I am and where I came from. My teaching is true, not because, like Moses, I declare that God spoke to me on Sinai, but because it exists in you too. Everyone who believes my commandments does so not because it is I who speak, but because our common Father draws him to Himself; and my teaching will give him life at the last day. It is written in the prophets that all men shall be taught of God. Everyone who understands the Father, and learns to know His will, yields himself to my teaching.

No one has ever seen the Father, but he that is of God has seen and sees Him.

He who believes in me (in my teaching) has everlasting life. My teaching is the food of life. Your fathers ate manna, food sent from heaven, and yet died. But the true food of life which descends from heaven is such that he who feeds on it will not die. And my teaching is this food of life that has descended from heaven. He who feeds on it lives forever. And this food which I teach is my body which I give for the life of mankind.

The Jews did not at all understand what he said, and began to dispute as to how it was possible to give one's body for the life of men, and why.

And Jesus said to them: If you do not give your body for the life of the spirit there will be no life in you. He who does not give his body for the life of the spirit has no real life. Only that in me which gives up the body for the spirit has real life. And therefore our bodies are truly food for the real life. Only that in me which consumes my body, that which gives up the bodily life for the true life - is really I - it is in me, and I am in it. And as I live in the body by the will of the Father, so that which lives in me lives by my will.

And some of his pupils when they heard this, said: These are hard words, and it is difficult to understand them. Jn vi 60 - 61

And Jesus said to them: Your minds are so confused, that my saying about what man was, is, and always will be, seems to you difficult. Man is a spirit in the flesh, and the spirit alone gives life - the flesh does not give life. In the words that seem to you so difficult I said no more than that the spirit is life. Jn vi 63

Afterwards Jesus chose seventy men from among those near him, and sent them to places he himself wished to go to. He said to them: Lk x 1 - 3

Many men do not know the blessing of real life. I am sorry for them all, and wish to teach them.

But as a husbandman cannot himself reap his whole harvest, so I, too, cannot do all that is needed. Go you to different towns and proclaim everywhere the fulfillment of the will of the Father.

Say: The will of the Father is this: not to be angry, not to lust, not to take oaths, not to resist evil, and not to make any distinction between people. And accordingly fulfill these laws yourselves in everything.

Mt x 16
Lk x
4 - 5
I send you like sheep among wolves. Be wise as serpents and pure as doves. Above all, have nothing of your own; take nothing with you, neither wallet, nor bread, nor money, only the clothes you wear and shoes. Make no distinction between people; do not choose out the Mt x 12 people with whom you will stay. But stay in whatever house you first come to. When you enter a house, greet the master. If he take you in, stay there; if not, go to another house.

Mt x
22 - 23
For what you will say they will hate you and fall upon you and drive you away. But when you are driven out go to another village, and if you are driven from there, go to yet another. You will be pursued as wolves pursue sheep, but do not be afraid, endure to the last hour. They will take you to the Courts and try you, and will flog you and take you before the authorities for Mt x 19 you to justify yourselves before them. But do not be afraid when you are taken to the Courts, and do not prepare what you will say: the spirit of the Mt x 23 Father in you will tell you what to say. Before you have passed through all the towns some people will understand your teaching and turn to it.

Mt x 27
So be not afraid. What is hidden in men's souls will come forth. Mt x 26 What you will say to two or three will spread among thousands. Above Mt x
28 - 31 all, do not be afraid of those who can kill your body. They can do nothing to your souls, so fear them not. Fear rather that which can destroy both body and soul by the non-fulfillment of the Father's will - fear that. Five sparrows are sold for a farthing, but even they do not die without the Father's will. And no hair falls from the head without the Father's will. So what have you to fear if you live in that will?

Mt x 34
Not everyone will believe in my teaching. And those who do not believe will hate it because it deprives them of what they love. So Lk xii 49 dissensions will come from my teaching. It will kindle the world like Lk xii
51-53 a fire, and from it strife must arise. There will be dissension in every house, father against son, mother against daughter. Families will hate those members who understand my teaching, and will kill them. For to Lk xiv 26 him who understands my teaching there will be no meaning in 'father', or 'mother', or 'wife', or 'children', or 'property'.

Then the learned Orthodox gathered at Jerusalem and went to Jesus who was in a village near by. A crowd of people had thronged into the house where he was and stood around it.

Mk iii 22
Mk iii 20

The Orthodox began to speak to the people, telling them not to listen to the teaching of Jesus. They said that he was possessed of a devil, and that if men lived by his commandments there would be still more evil in the world than now. They said that he drove out evil by evil means.

Mk vii 24 - 29

Jesus called them to him and said: You say that I drive out evil by evil. But no power destroys itself. If it destroyed itself it would cease to exist. You try to drive out evil by threats, executions, and murders, but evil still exists precisely because it cannot fight against itself. I do not drive out evil by evil as you try to.

I drive out evil by calling on men to fulfill the will of the Father's spirit which gives life to all men. Five commandments express the will of that spirit, which gives happiness and life. And they therefore destroy evil. That is a proof that they are true.

If men were not sons of one spirit it would not be possible to overcome evil, just as it is not possible to enter a strong man's house and rob it. To rob his house it is necessary first to bind the strong man. And men are bound by their unity in the spirit of life.

And so I say to you that all mistakes of men and every false opinion shall escape punishment, but false interpretations of the holy spirit, which gives life to all, will not be forgiven.

Mk vii 31 - 32

If anyone speaks ill of a man it may not be counted against him, but if anyone speaks against the holy spirit in man, that cannot pass without harm to him. Abuse me as much as you like, but do not decry the commandments of life I have disclosed to you. It cannot pass harmlessly for a man if he calls what is good - evil.

Man must be at one with the spirit of life. He who is not at one with it is against it. Man must serve the spirit of life and goodness in all men, and not in himself alone.

Mt xii 30

Either you believe life and happiness to be good for the whole world, and should then love life and happiness for all men, or you believe life and happiness to be evil, and should then not love them even for yourself. Either you consider a tree good and its fruit good, or else you consider the tree bad and its fruit bad. For a tree is valued by its fruit.

Mt xii 33

VI: THE FALSE LIFE

To obtain true life, man must on earth resign
the false life of the flesh and live by the spirit.

"AS IN HEAVEN SO ON EARTH"

Lk viii 19

Once his mother and brothers came to Jesus, and could not get to him because there were so many around him. A man seeing them went Mt xii 46 - 47 to Jesus and said: Your family, your mother and brothers, are standing outside wanting to see you.

Lk viii 21

But Jesus said: My mother and my brothers are those who have understood the will of the Father, and do it.

Lk xi 27 - 28

And a woman exclaimed: Blessed is the womb that bore you and the breasts that you have sucked!

And Jesus replied: Only they are blessed who have understood the spirit of the Father and keep it.

Lk ix 57 - 58

And a man said to Jesus: I will follow you wherever you may go.

Jesus answered him: There is nowhere for you to follow me to: I have neither house nor any place to live in. The beasts have their dens and their lairs, but man is at home everywhere if he lives by the spirit.

Mk iv 35

Mk iv 37 - 38

It happened once that Jesus was sailing with his pupils in a boat. He said: Let us cross to the other side. A storm arose on the lake and the boat began to fill so that it nearly sank. But Jesus lay in the stern and slept. They woke him and said: Master, is it nothing to you if we are Mk iv, 40 drowned? And when the storm subsided he said: Why are you so timid? You have no faith in the life of the spirit.

Lk ix 59 - 62

To one man Jesus said: Follow me.

But the man replied: I have a father who is old; let me first bury him and then I will follow you.

And Jesus said to him: Let the dead bury the dead, but if you wish really to live fulfill the Father's will and publish it.

Another man said: I wish to be your pupil and will fulfill the Father's will as you command, but let me first arrange my family affairs.

And Jesus said to him: If a ploughman looks back he cannot plough. As long as you look back you cannot plough. You must forget everything except the furrow you are driving and only then can you plough. If you consider what may befall your bodily life you cannot live, because you have not understood the real life.

After this it happened that Jesus went with his pupils into a village, Lk x 38 - 42 and a woman named Martha asked him into her house. She had a sister, Mary, who sat at Jesus' feet and listened to his teaching, while Martha was busy preparing a good meal for them.

And Martha went up to Jesus and said: Do you not see that my sister leaves me to do all the work? Tell her to help me with it.

In reply Jesus said to her: Martha, Martha! You busy yourself and are anxious about many things, but only one thing is needful; Mary has chosen that one necessary thing which no one shall take from her. The one thing needful for life is food for the soul.

And Jesus said to them all: Lk ix 23 - 25

He who wishes to follow me, let him put aside his own will and be ready to endure all hardships and sufferings of the flesh throughout his life; only then can he follow me. He who wishes to take heed for his bodily life will destroy his true life, but he who obeys the will of the Father, even though he may destroy his bodily life, will save his true life. And what profit is it to a man if he gains the whole world but destroys or harms his true life?

And he said: Beware of riches, for your life does not depend on Lk xii 15 - 21 possessing more than others.

There was once a rich man who had a large harvest. And he thought to himself, I will rebuild my barns and put up larger ones and gather all my wealth into them, and I will say to my soul: There, my soul, you have all you desire; rest, eat, drink, and live for your pleasure. But God said to him: Foolish man, tonight your soul will be taken and all that you have stored up will go to others.

So it is with everyone who provides for his bodily life and does not live in God.

And Jesus said to them: You tell me that Pilate slew the Galileans. Lk xiii 2 - 8 Were those Galileans any worse than others, that this happened to them? Not at all. We are all such, and we also shall all perish unless we find salvation from death. Or were those eighteen men who were crushed by a falling tower, worse than all the other people of Jerusalem? Not at all. If we do not save ourselves from death, today or tomorrow we too shall perish.

If we have not yet perished as they did, we must think of our position thus:

A man had an apple-tree in his garden and he came and looked at the tree and saw there was no fruit on it. And he said to the gardener: This is the third year I have been here and found that apple tree always barren. It must be cut down, for it only takes up space uselessly. But the gardener said: Let us wait awhile, master. I will dig round it, manure it, and we will see next summer. Perhaps it will bear fruit, but if not, then cut it down.

So we, too, while we live in the flesh and do not bear fruit of the life of the spirit, are barren apple trees. Only by someone's mercy are we left for another year. But if we do not bear fruit we too shall perish, like him who rebuilt his barns, like the Galileans, like the eighteen men crushed by the falling tower, and like all who do not bear fruit, perishing and dying for ever.

Lk xii
54 - 56

To understand this no wisdom is necessary; everyone can see it for himself. Not only in domestic affairs but in all that goes on in the world we can reason and guess what is coming. If the wind is from the west, we say: It will rain, and so it happens. But if there is wind from the south, we say: It will be fine, and so it happens. How is it that we can tell the weather, but cannot foresee that we shall all die and perish, and that the only salvation for us is in the life of the spirit, the fulfillment of its will?

Lk xiv
25 - 33

And many people followed Jesus, and he again said to them all:

He who would be my follower, let him put out of mind his father, mother, wife, children, brothers, sisters, and all his property, and let him at all times be ready for anything. Only he who does what I do and follows my teaching can save himself from death.

For every man before beginning anything considers whether what he would do is profitable; if it seems profitable he does it, but if it seems unprofitable he will abandon it. Every man who builds a house first sits down and reckons how much it will cost, how much he has, and whether he can finish it; that it may not happen that having begun to build he should be unable to finish, and so be laughed at.

So also he who wishes to live the life of the flesh should first consider how he can finish what he is engaged on.

Every king who wishes to go to war will first consider whether he can go against twenty thousand men with only ten thousand. If he sees that he cannot, he will send an ambassador to make peace, and will not go to war.

So let every man, before giving himself to the life of the flesh, bethink himself whether he can resist death or whether death is stronger than he, and whether he had not better make peace at once.

Each of you should first reckon all that he considers his own: family, money, and property. When he has considered what all this avails him, and understands that it avails him nothing, only then can he be my follower.

And hearing this, a man said: That is well if there be a life of the spirit. But what if we give up everything and there is no such life? Lk xiv 15 - 16

To that Jesus replied: Not so. Everyone knows the life of the spirit. You all know it. You do not practice what you know, not because you doubt, but because you are diverted from the true life by false cares and excuse yourself from it.

This is like what you do: A master prepared a dinner and sent to invite guests, but they began to decline. One said: I have bought some land and must go to see it. Another said: I have bought some oxen and must try them. A third said: I have married and must give a wedding feast. And the servants came and told the master that no one would come. Then the master sent his servants to call in the poor, and they did not refuse but came. And when they had come there was still room to spare, so the master sent to call in others, saying: Go and persuade everyone you meet to come to my dinner, that there may be still more guests. But those who refused because they were busy missed the dinner. Lk xiv 18 - 23

All men know that the fulfillment of the will of the Father gives life, but they do not accept his invitation because they are drawn away by the guile of riches.

He who gives up false transitory riches for true life in accord with the Father's will, acts as a clever steward did.

There was a steward to a rich master. This steward saw that his master would soon dismiss him and he would be left without food or shelter. And he thought to himself. This is what I will do. I will secretly give away some of my master's goods to the peasants and reduce their debts, and then if my master sends me away the peasants will remember my kindness and will help me. And he did so. He called the peasants who were in debt to his master, and re-wrote their quittances. For him who owed a hundred he made it fifty; instead of sixty he put down twenty, and for the others in the same way. When the master heard of this he said to himself: My steward has acted cleverly, for he saw he would have been left with nothing. He has caused me loss, but he has acted cleverly for himself. Lk xvi 1 - 3 Lk xvi 5 - 6 Lk xvi 8 -12

For in the bodily life we all understand what is advantageous, but in regard to the life of the spirit we do not wish to understand. We should give away the transitory and false riches of this life in order to I obtain the life of the spirit. If we grudge such trifles as riches for the life of the spirit, we shall not receive it. If we do not give up the false life our true life will not be given us.

It is not possible to serve two masters at once - God and riches: the will of the Father and your own will. You must serve either the one or the other.

Lk xvi
14 - 17

The Orthodox heard this, and as they loved wealth they ridiculed him.

But he said to them: You think that because you are honored by men for your wealth you are really honorable. It is not so. God does not look at the exterior, but at the heart. That which is esteemed among men is despicable in God's sight. Even now the Kingdom of God is attainable on earth, and they who enter it are great. And it is not the rich who enter that kingdom, but those who have nothing. This always was so, and is so by your law and by Moses and the prophets. Listen how the rich the and poor stand, even in your belief.

Lk xvi
19 - 31

There was a rich man, who dressed in fine clothes and went to amuse himself and to make merry every day. And there was a beggar named Lazarus, covered with sores, who came to the rich man's yard to see if some scraps might not be left over from the rich man's feast; but Lazarus did not get even these, the rich man's dogs ate them all up and even licked Lazarus's sores. And both Lazarus and the rich man died. And when in hell the rich man saw Abraham afar off, and the beggar Lazarus sitting with him. And the rich man cried: Father Abraham, Lazarus the beggar is sitting with you, who used to lie outside my fence. I dare not trouble you; but send Lazarus the beggar to me: let him but dip his finger in water and cool my tongue, for I am burning in the fire. But Abraham said: Why should I send Lazarus into the fire to you? In the world you had what you wished, but Lazarus only had sorrow, so now he must be comforted. And even though I might like to do it, I cannot send him to you, for there is a great gulf between us and you which cannot be crossed. We are living and you are dead. Then the rich man said: Well, Father Abraham, at least send Lazarus to my house. I have five brothers and am sorry for them. Let him tell them everything, and show them how harmful riches are, or they too may fall into this torment. But Abraham said: They know already that it is harmful. Moses and all the prophets have told them so. But the rich man said: Still, it would be better if someone were to rise from the dead and go to them, they would then bethink themselves. But Abraham said: If they do not listen to Moses and the prophets, they would not listen even to one who rose from the dead.

That a man ought to share with his brother and do good to all men, is known to everyone. The whole law of Moses and the prophets only says that. You know it, but because you love riches you cannot obey it.

And a rich Orthodox official came to Jesus and said to him: You are a good teacher. What must I do to obtain everlasting life? Mk x 17 - 25

Jesus said to him: Why do you call me good? Only the father is good. If you wish to have life, fulfill the commandments.

The official said: There are many commandments - which must I fulfill?

And Jesus said: Do not kill, do not lust, do not lie, do not steal. Also, honor your Father and fulfill his will, and love your neighbor as yourself.

And the Orthodox official said: I have kept all those commandments since I was a child; but I ask what else must I do according to your teaching?

Jesus looked at him and at his rich clothes, smiled, and said: One little thing you have not yet done. You have not fulfilled everything, as you say. If you wish to fulfill the commandments: not to kill, not to lust, not to steal, not to lie, and the chief command, to love your neighbor as yourself - then sell all your possessions at once and give to the poor. Then you will fulfill the Father's will.

Hearing this, the official frowned and went away, for he was loathe to part with his possessions.

And Jesus said to his pupils: As you see, it is quite impossible to be rich and to fulfill the Father's will.

The pupils were horrified at these words, but Jesus repeated them again, and said: Yes, children, it is impossible for him who has riches to be in the Father's will. A camel can pass through the eye of a needle sooner than he who trusts in riches fulfill the will of the Father. Lk xviii 25 - 27

And they were still more horrified and said: How then can one preserve one's life?

But he said: To a man it seems that he cannot support his life without property, but God preserves a man's life without property.

Jesus was once passing through the town of Jericho. And a prominent tax-farmer was there, a rich man named Zacchaeus, who had heard of Jesus' teaching and believed in it, and when he learnt that Jesus was in Jericho he wished to see him. But there was such a crowd round Jesus that it was impossible to push through to him. Zacchaeus was a small man, so he ran ahead and climbed a tree that he might see Jesus as he went past. When passing the tree Jesus saw him, and knowing that he believed in his teaching said: Come down from the tree and go home. I Lk xix 1 - 10 will come to you. Zacchaeus climbed down, ran home, made ready to welcome Jesus, and received him joyfully.

The people disapproved of this and said of Jesus: Why, he has gone to a taxfarmer's, to a scoundrel's house!

At that very time Zacchaeus was saying to Jesus: See, Master, what I will do: I will give half my property to the poor, and out of what is left I will repay fourfold to all whom I have wronged.

And Jesus said: You have saved yourself. You were dead but have come to life; you were lost, but have found yourself; for you have done as Abraham did when by being ready to kill his own son he showed his faith. For herein is the whole life of man; to find and save that which is perishing in his soul. A sacrifice cannot be measured by its size.

Mk xii
41 - 44

It happened once that Jesus was sitting with his pupils near a collecting box. People were placing contributions in the box for God's service. Rich men went up to the box and put in much, and a poor widow came and put in two farthings.

And Jesus pointed to her and said: See, this poor widow, a beggar-woman, has given two farthings, and she has given more than all the others. For they gave what they did not need, while she has given all she had; she has put in her whole substance.

Mk xxvi
6 - 13

It happened that Jesus was at the house of Simon the leper.

And a woman came into the house and she had a jar of precious oil, worth thirty pounds. Jesus was saying to his pupils that his death was near, and the woman heard this and was sorry for him, and to show him her love poured oil on his head. And she forgot everything, and broke her jar, and anointed both his head and his feet, and poured out all the oil.

And the pupils began to discuss it, and said she had acted badly. And Judas, who afterwards betrayed Jesus, said: See how much she has wasted. That oil might have been sold for thirty pounds, with which many poor people could have been clothed. And the pupils began blaming the woman, who was abashed and did not know whether she had done well or ill.

Then Jesus said: You are wrong to trouble the woman; she has indeed done a good deed, and you are wrong to speak about the poor. If you want to do good to them, do so - they are always there. But why speak of them now? If you pity the poor, go with your pity and do them good. But this woman has pitied me and done good truly, for she has given away all that she had. Which of you can tell what is needful and what is not? How do you know that there was no need to anoint me with the oil? She has poured it on me to prepare my body for burial, and for that it was wanted. She has truly done the will of the Father by forgetting herself and pitying another. She forgot her worldly reckonings and gave away all that she had.

And Jesus said: My teaching is to do the Father's will, and His will can only be fulfilled by deeds, and not by words only. If a man's son keeps saying, 'I will, I will', to his father's bidding, but does not do what his father says, then he does not fulfill his father's will. But if another son says: 'I do not wish to obey', but then goes and does his father's bidding - he indeed fulfills his father's will. So also with men: not he is in the Father's will who says: 'I am in the Father's will', but he who does what the Father wishes.

Mt xxi 28 -29

VII: I AND THE FATHER ARE ONE

The true food of everlasting life is the fulfillment Of the Father's will

"GIVE US OUR DAILY BREAD"

Jn vii
1 -3
After that the Jews wished to condemn Jesus to death, and he went away into Galilee and lived with his relations.

Jn vii 5
Jn vii
3 - 4
The Jewish feast of tabernacles was come, and the brothers of Jesus prepared to go to the feast, and called him to go with them. They did not believe in his teaching and said to him:You say that the Jewish service of God is wrong and that you know the real way to serve God by deeds. If you really think that no one but you knows how to serve God come with us to the feast. Many people will be there and you can declare before them all that the teaching of Moses is wrong. If they all believe you, then your pupils also will see that you are right. Why hide yourself? You say that our service is wrong, and that you know the true service of God: well then, show it to everybody.

Jn vii
6 - 12
And Jesus said: You have a special time and place in which to serve God, but for me there is none. I work for God everywhere and always. That is just what I show to people. I show them that their service of God is wrong and that is why they hate me. Go you to the feast, and I will go when I am ready.

And his brothers went, but he remained behind, and only went up at the middle of the feast.

The Jews were shocked that he did not honor their feast and delayed coming to it, and they disputed about his teaching. Some said that he was right, while others said that he only disturbed the people.

Jn vii
14 - 19
In the middle of the feast Jesus went into the Temple and began to teach the people that their service of God was wrong, and that God should be served not in a temple and by sacrifices, but in the spirit and by deeds.

They all listened to him and wondered that he, an unlearned man, should have such wisdom. And Jesus, knowing that all wondered at his wisdom, said to them: My teaching is not my own, but His that sent me. If any man wishes to do the will of the spirit that sent us into life, he will know that I have not invented this teaching but that it is of God. For a man who invents from himself follows his own imagination, but he who seeks to know the mind of Him that sent him is true and there is no falsehood in him.

Your law of Moses is not the Father's law, and so those who follow it do not fulfill the Father's law, but do evil and tell falsehoods. I teach you the fulfillment of the will of the Father alone. In my teaching there can be no contradictions, but your written Mosaic law is full of contradictions. Do not judge by externals, but by the spirit. And some said: They said he was a false prophet, but he condemns the law and no one says anything to him. Perhaps he is really a true prophet and even the rulers have recognized him. But there is one reason for not believing him: it is written that when God's messenger shall come no one will know whence he came, but we know where this man was born and we know his whole family. ^{Jn vii 21 - 29}

The people still did not understand his teaching, and still sought proofs.

Then Jesus said to them: You know me, and where I came from in the body, but you do not know where I come from in the spirit. You do not know Him from whom I come in spirit, and that is the one thing it is necessary to know. If I had said: 'I am the Christ', you would have believed me, the man, but you would not have believed the Father who is in me and in you. You should believe in the Father only.

For the short space of my life I point out to you the path to that source of life from which I have come. But you ask of me proofs, and wish to condemn me. If you do not know that path, then when I am no longer here you will not be able to find it. You should not judge me but should follow me. He who does what I say will know whether what I say is true. He for whom the life of the flesh has not become merely food for the spirit, he who does not seek truth as a thirsty man seeks for water, cannot understand me. He who thirsts for truth, let him come to me and drink. And he who believes my teaching will obtain true life. He will receive the life of the spirit. ^{Jn vii 33 - 52}

And many believed his teaching and said: What he says is true, and is of God. Others did not understand him, and were always seeking in the prophecies for proofs that he was sent from God. And many disputed with him but no one was able to controvert him. The Orthodox teachers of the law sent their assistants to contend with him, but these assistants returned to them and said: We can do nothing with him.

And the chief priest said: How is it you have not convicted him?

They replied: No one ever spoke as he does.

Then the Orthodox said: It signifies nothing that you cannot refute him and that the people believe his teaching. We do not believe it and none of the rulers believe it. The people are accursed, they always were stupid and ignorant, and will believe anyone.

But Nicodemus, to whom Jesus had explained his teaching, said to the chief priests: A man should not be condemned without being heard, and without understanding what he teaches.

But they said to him: There is nothing to hear or to understand. We know that no prophet can come from Galilee.

Jn viii
12 - 14

Another time Jesus spoke to the Orthodox and said: There can be no proof of the truth of my teaching, just as you cannot have an illumination of light. My teaching is the real light by which people see what is good and what is bad, and so it is impossible to prove my teaching; everything else is proved by it. He who follows me will not be in darkness but will have life. Life and enlightenment are one and the same.

But the Orthodox said: It is only you who say this.

And he replied: If I alone say it, still I am right, for I know whence I come and whither I go. In my teaching life has a meaning, but according to yours it has none. Besides, not I alone teach this, but my Father, the spirit, teaches it too.

Jn viii
18 - 19

They said: Where is your Father?

Jn viii 21

He replied: You do not understand my teaching or you would know my Father. You do not know whence you are nor whither you go.

I show you the way, but instead of following me you discuss who I am; and so you cannot reach that salvation and life to which I wish to lead you. And you will perish if you remain in this error and do not follow me.

Jn viii
24 - 26

The Jews asked: Who are you?

He said: I told you when I first began to teach: I am the son of man, acknowledging the spirit as my Father, and what I have understood from him I tell to the world. When you exalt the son of man in yourselves you will know what I am, because I do and speak not of myself as a man, but what the Father has taught me. He who sent me is always in me and will not leave me, for I do His will. He who keeps to my understanding of life and fulfills the will of the Father will be truly taught by me. To know the truth you must do good to men. He who does harm to men loves the darkness and goes towards it; he who does good to men goes to the light. So to understand my teaching you must do good. He who does good will know the truth; he will be free from evil, from death. For everyone who errs becomes the slave of his error.

Jn viii
28 - 29

Jn viii
31 - 32

Jn viii
34 - 44

And as a slave does not always live in his master's house while the master's son does, so a man if he errs in life and becomes the slave of his errors does not live always, but dies. Only he who is in the truth remains always living. To know truth is to be a son and not a slave. If you err, you will be slaves and will die: but if you are in the truth you will be free sons and will live.

You say of yourselves that you are sons of Abraham, and that you know the truth. Yet you wish to kill me because you do not understand my teaching. And it comes to this, that I speak what I have understood from my Father while you wish to do what you have understood from your father.

They said: Our father is Abraham.

Jesus said to them: If you were the sons of Abraham you would do his deeds. But you wish to kill me because I have told you what I have learnt from God. Abraham did not act like that. You do not serve God, but serve another father.

They said to him: We are not bastards, we are all sons of one Father, we are all God's children.

And Jesus said to them: If your father were one with me you would love me, for I came forth from the Father; I was not born of myself. You are not children of one Father with me, so you do not understand my words and my understanding of life finds no place in you. If I am of the Father and you are of the same Father, then you cannot wish to kill me. If you wish to kill me, we are not of the same Father.

I am from the Father of goodness, God: but you are from the father of evil, the devil. You wish to do the lusts of your father who always was a murderer and a liar with no truth in him. If he, the devil, says anything, he says not what is common to all, but what is his own, and he is the father of lies. So you are servants of the devil and are his children.

You see how plainly you are convicted of error. If I err, convict me; Jn viii 46 but if there is no error in me why do you not believe me.

And the Jews began to revile him and to say that he was possessed. Jn viii 48 - 59

He said: I am not possessed. I honor thy Father, and you wish to kill me, which shows that you are not my brothers but sons of another father.

It is not I who affirm that I am right, but the truth that speaks for me. And so I repeat to you: he who comprehends my teaching and performs it shall not see death.

And the Jews said: Now, were we not right in saying that you are a Samaritan and have a devil? You convict yourself!

The prophets died, so did Abraham, yet you say that he who fulfills your teaching shall not see death. Abraham died, and will you not die? Or are you greater than Abraham?

The Jews discussed what he - Jesus of Galilee - was, whether he was an important or an unimportant prophet, and forgot that he had told them that he said nothing of himself as a man but spoke of the spirit that was within him.

And Jesus said: I do not make myself out to be anything. If I spoke of myself, of what I imagine, then all I might say would be of no importance. But there is that source of all things which you call God. It is of that I speak. You have not known, and do not know, the true God. But I know Him and if I said I do not know Him I should be a liar like you. I know Him and know and fulfill His will.

Your father Abraham saw and rejoiced at what I understand.

The Jews said: You are not yet thirty: how could you be alive in Abraham's day?

He replied: Before Abraham existed there was the understanding of good that I tell you of.

Then the Jews picked up stones to throw at him, but he escaped.

Jn ix 1 - 5

And on the road, Jesus saw a man who had no understanding from the time of his birth.

And his pupils asked him: Who is at fault that this man is without understanding since his birth? He, or his parents for not having taught him?

And Jesus replied: Neither his parents nor he are at fault. It is God's doing, that there may be light where there was darkness. If I have a teaching, it is the light of the world.

Jn ix 6 - 11

And Jesus explained to the ignorant man that he was a son of God in the spirit, and on receiving this teaching the ignorant man was conscious of light. Those who had known him previously did not recognize him. Though resembling what he had been, he had now become another man. But he said: I am he, and Jesus has shown me that I am a son of God, and the light has reached me, so that now I see what I used not to see.

Jn ix 13 - 21

This man was taken to the Orthodox teachers; and it was on a Saturday.

The Orthodox asked him how he had come to understand what he had not seen before.

He said: I do not know how; I only know that now I understand everything.

They said: You do not understand in a godly way, for Jesus did this on a Saturday, and besides, a layman cannot enlighten people.

And they began to dispute, and asked of the man who had been enlightened: What do you think of Jesus?

He said: I think he is a prophet.

But the Jews did not believe that he had been ignorant and was now enlightened, so they called his parents and asked them: Is this your son, who has been ignorant since his birth? How is it he has now become enlightened?

His parents said: We know that he is our son and that he was ignorant from his birth, but how he has become enlightened we do not know. He is of age, you should ask him.

The Orthodox called the man a second time, and said: Pray to our God, the real God. The man who enlightened you is a layman, and is not sent by God. We are sure of that. Jn ix 24 - 31

And the man who had been enlightened said: Whether he is from God or not I do not know. But I know that I used not to see the light and that I see it now.

The Orthodox again asked: What did he do to you when he enlightened you?

He replied: I have told you already, but you do not believe. If you wish to be his pupils I will tell you again.

They began to revile him and said: You are his pupil, but we are the pupils of Moses. God Himself spoke to Moses, but we do not even know whence this man is.

And the man answered: It is strange that he has enlightened me and yet you do not know whence he is. God does not hear sinners but hears those who honour Him and do His will. It can never be that one who is not from God could enlighten an ignorant man. If he were not from God he could do nothing. Jn ix 33 - 34

The Orthodox were angry at this, and said: You are altogether sunk in delusions and yet you want to teach us. And they drove him away.

And Jesus said: My teaching is an awakening to life. He who believes in my teaching, though he die in the flesh, remains living, and everyone who lives and believes in me will not die. Jn xi 25 - 26

And yet a third time Jesus taught the people. He said: Men accept my teaching not because I myself prove it. It is impossible to prove the truth. The truth itself proves all else. But men accept my teaching because there is no other that is native to them and promises life. Jn x 2 - 3

My teaching is to men like the familiar voice of the shepherd to the sheep, when he comes to them through the door and gathers them to

Jn x 5

lead them to pasture. No one believes your teaching, for it is foreign to them, and they see your own lusts in it. Men feel with you as sheep do at the sight of someone who does not enter by the door but climbs over

Jn x
7 - 14

the fence: the sheep do not know him, and feel that he is a robber. My teaching is the one true teaching, like the one door for the sheep. All your teachings of the law of Moses are false, as thieves and robbers are to the sheep. He who yields to my teaching will find true life - just as the sheep go forth and find food if they follow the shepherd. A thief only comes to steal, rob, and destroy…but the shepherd comes to give life. And my teaching alone promises to give true life.

There are shepherds for whom the sheep are their life and who are ready to give their life for the sheep. These are the true shepherds. But there are hirelings who care nothing for the sheep, because they are hirelings and the sheep are not theirs. If a wolf comes they abandon the sheep and run away, and the wolf devours them. They are false shepherds. So also there are false teachers who care nothing for the life of people, but true teachers give up their lives for the life of men.

Jn x
17 - 18

I am such a teacher. My teaching is this - to give up one's life for the life of men. No one will take my life from me, but I myself freely give it up for men to receive true life. That commandment I have received

Jn x 15

from my Father. As my Father knows me so also I know Him, and

Jn x 17

therefore I lay down my life for men. And my Father loves me because I fulfill His commandment.

Jn x 16

And all men, not only those here and now, but all men, shall understand my voice; and they will all come together in me and all men shall be one and their teaching one.

Jn x
24 - 38

And the Jews surrounded him and said: What you say is hard to understand and does not agree with our scriptures. Do not torment us, but tell us simply and plainly whether you are the Messiah, who according to our scriptures should come into the world.

Jesus answered them: I have already told you who I am, but you do not believe. If you do not believe my words then believe my works; by them you can understand who I am and for what I have come.

You do not believe because you do not follow me. He who follows me and does what I say will understand me. And those who understand my teaching and fulfill it, receive true life. My Father has united them with me, and no one can disunite us. I and the Father are one.

And the Jews were offended at this and took up stones to kill him.

But he said to them: I have shown you many good works and have disclosed the teaching of my Father. For which of these good works do you wish to stone me?

They said: Not for your good works do we wish to stone you, but because you, a man, make yourself God.

And Jesus replied to them: The same is written in your scriptures where it is said that God Himself said to the wicked rulers: 'Ye are Gods.' If He called even wicked men Gods, why do you consider it blasphemous to call what God in his love has sent into the world, 'the son of God'' Every man in the spirit is a son of', God. If I do not live in God's way, then do not believe that I am a son of God. But if I live after God's way then believe by my life that I am with the Father, and understand that the Father is in me and I in Him.

And the Jews began to dispute. Some said that he was possessed and others said: A man who is possessed cannot enlighten men. Jn x 20 - 21

And they did not know what to do with him and could not condemn him. And he again went beyond the Jordan and stayed there. Jn x 39 - 42

And many believed in his teaching and said that it was true as the teaching of John was. Therefore many believed in it.

And Jesus once asked his pupils: Tell me, how do people understand my teaching about the son of God and the son of man? Mt xvi 13 - 18

They said: Some understand it like the teaching of John: others like the prophecies of Isaiah: others again say it is like the teaching of Jeremiah. They understand that you are a prophet.

And he asked them: But how do you understand my teaching?

And Simon Peter said to him: I think your teaching is that you are the chosen son of the God of life. You teach that God is the life within man.

And Jesus said to him: Happy are you, Simon, that you have understood this. No man could disclose it to you: you have understood it because the divine spirit in you has disclosed it to you. Not human understanding and not I by my words have disclosed it to you, but God, my Father, has disclosed it to you directly. And on this is founded the society of men for whom there is no death.

VIII: LIFE IS NOT TEMPORAL

Therefore true life must be lived in the present.

"EACH DAY"

Mt x
38 - 39

Jesus said: He who is not prepared to suffer all bodily sufferings and deprivations has not understood me. He who obtains all that is best for his bodily life destroys the true life. But he who sacrifices his bodily life in fulfilling my teaching will receive the true life.

Mt ix 27

And at those words, Peter said to him: See, we have obeyed you, have thrown off all ties and property, and have followed you. What reward shall we receive for this?

Mk x
29 - 31

Jesus said to him: Everyone who has given up home, sisters, brothers, father, mother, wife, children, or lands, for my teaching, shall receive a hundredfold more than sisters, brothers, and fields, and all that is needful in this life, and besides that obtains also life beyond the bounds of time. There are no rewards in the kingdom of heaven, the kingdom of heaven is its own aim and reward. In the kingdom of heaven all are equal, there is neither first nor last.

Mt xx
1 - 3

For the kingdom of heaven is like this: The master of a house went in the morning to hire laborers for his garden. He hired them at a penny a day, and set them to work. At midday he went again and hired more laborers and sent them to work in his garden; towards evening he hired some more, and sent them to work. And he agreed with them all at a

Mt xx
8 - 16

penny. When the time came for payment, the master had them all paid alike: first those who were hired last, and afterwards those who had been hired first. When those who had been hired first saw that those hired last received a penny each, they thought they would receive more, but they also were paid a penny. They took it and said: How is it that the others who worked only one shift and we who worked all four shifts receive the same? That is not fair. But the master came and said: Why are you dissatisfied? Have I wronged you? I have given you what we agreed on. Our agreement was for a penny. Take your pay and go. If I give to these last the same as to you, have I not the right to do what I will with my own? Or are you envious because you see that I am good?

In the kingdom of heaven there is no first or last - it is the same for all.

Mt xx 20
Mk x 35

After this, two of his pupils, James and John, came to Jesus and said: Teacher, promise us that you will give us what we ask.

He said: What do you want?

Mt xx
21 - 28

They said: That we may be equal with you.

Jesus said to them: You do not know what you are asking. You can live as I do and can cleanse yourselves from the fleshly life like me, but it is not in my power to make you like myself. Each man can by his own efforts enter the kingdom of the Father by submitting to His power and fulfilling His will.

On hearing this the other pupils grew angry with the two brothers for having wished to be equal to their teacher, and chiefs among the pupils.

But Jesus called them, and said: If you brothers, John and James, have asked me to make you such as I am in order to be chief among my pupils, you made a mistake; and it you, my other pupils, were angry with them for wishing to be above you, then you also made a mistake. In the world, kings and governors reckon by seniority, that they may rule the people: but among you there can be neither senior nor junior.

Among you, to be more than another you must be the servant of all. Among you, let him who wishes to be first consider himself last. For the will of the Father is that the son of man should live not to be served but to serve all and give up his bodily life as a ransom for the life of the spirit.

Jesus said to the people: The Father seeks to save that which is perishing, He rejoices over it as a shepherd rejoices when he finds a lost sheep. If one sheep is lost, the shepherd will leave ninety-nine and go to save the lost one. And if a woman loses a penny, she will sweep out the whole hut and seek till she finds it. The Father loves the son and calls him to himself.

Mt xviii
11 - 12

Lk xv 8
Lk xv 10

And he told them another parable showing that they who live according to God's will must not exalt themselves. He said: If you are invited to a dinner, do not seat yourself in a front place, or someone of more importance than you will come and the host will say to you: 'Leave your place and let someone better than yourself have it', and you will be put to shame. Take the lowest place: the host win then find you and call you to a higher one, and you will be honored.

Lk xiv
8 - 11

So also in the kingdom of God there is no room for pride. He who exalts himself, by so doing lowers himself; but he who humbles himself and considers himself unworthy, raises himself in the kingdom of God.

A man had two sons. The younger son said to his father: Father, give me my share of the property.

Lk xv
11 - 13

And the father gave him his share. The younger son took it, went to a far country, squandered it all, and fell into want. In that far country he became a swineherd, and he was so hungry that he ate acorns with the pigs. And he bethought himself of his life, and said: Why did I take my share and leave my father? He had plenty of everything, even his laborers were well fed. But here am I eating the same food as the pigs. I will go to my father, fall at his feet, and say: I have done wrong, father, and am unworthy to be your son. Take me back as a laborer. So

he thought, and he went to his father. And as he drew near, his father recognized him at a distance, and ran to meet him and embraced him and began to kiss him. And the son said: Father I am to blame before you, and am unworthy to be your son. But the father did not even listen, and said to the servants: Bring the best clothes and the best boots, quickly, and put them on him. And go and catch a fatted calf and kill it, and we will rejoice because this son of mine was dead and is now alive, was lost and is now found.

Then the elder brother came from the field, and as he drew near he heard sounds of music in the house and called a boy and said: Why are they making merry? And the boy said: Have you not heard that your brother has returned?

Your father is glad, and has had the fatted calf killed for joy that his son has come home. But the elder brother was vexed and did not go into the house. His father came out and called him, but he said to his father: Father, I have worked for you for many years, and have never disobeyed your orders, but you never killed a fatted calf for me. My younger brother left home and has squandered all his property with drunkards, and for him you have had a calf killed. And his father said: You are always with me and all that is mine is yours; you should not be vexed but rejoice that your brother who was dead has become alive again - was lost and is found.

A master planted a garden, cultivated it, and did everything to make it yield as much fruit as possible. And he sent laborers into the garden to work there, pay him for it according to agreement, and gather the fruit.

(The master is the Father; the garden the world; the laborers men. The Father has sent His son - the son of man - into the world only that men should make return of that - the understanding of life - which He implanted in them.) The time came when the master sent a servant to receive payment. (The Father has always told men that they must fulfill His will.) The laborers drove away the master's servant empty-handed and remained in the garden imagining that it was their own, and that they were settled in it of their own will. (Men reject reminders of the will of God, and continue to live each one for himself, imagining that the purpose of life is to serve the flesh.) Then the master sent, one after another, his chosen ones and finally his son, to remind the laborers of their debt. But they quite lost their reason and imagined that if they killed the master's son, who reminded them that the garden was not theirs, they would be left alone. So they killed him. Mk xii 6 - 8

(People do not like even a reminder of the spirit that lives in them and shows them that it is eternal and that they are not so; and as far as they can they have killed their consciousness of the spirit: they have wrapped the talent in a cloth and buried it.)

What then was the master to do? Simply to drive out those laborers and send others. Mt xxi 40 - 43

What is the Father to do? Sow until there is fruit. And this He does.

Men have not understood and do not understand that the consciousness of the spirit that is in them, and which they hide because it troubles them, brings life to them. They reject the stone on which everything rests. And they who do not take the life of the spirit as their foundation do not enter the kingdom of heaven and do not receive life. To have faith and to receive life it is necessary to understand your position and not expect rewards.

Then the pupils said to Jesus: Increase our faith in us; tell us what will make us believe more firmly in the life of the spirit, that we may not regret the life of the flesh. See how much has to be sacrificed, and continually sacrificed, for the life of the spirit. Yet you yourself say that there is no reward. Lk xvii 5 - 10

To this Jesus replied: You can readily believe that a great tree grows from a birch seed - if you had as much faith in the seed of the spirit which is within you and whence true life springs, you would not ask me to increase your faith.

Faith does not consist in believing something wonderful, but it consists in understanding your position and where salvation lies. If you understand your position you will not expect rewards but will believe in that which has been entrusted to you.

When a master returns from the field with his laborers, he does not seat them at table but bids them see to the cattle, and get his supper ready, and only afterwards says to them: Sit down and eat and drink. The master does not thank the laborer for having done what he ought to do. And the laborer, if he understands that he is a laborer, is not offended but does his work believing that he will receive his due.

So you too should fulfill the will of the Father and remember that we are unprofitable servants who have only done what we ought to, and not expect rewards but be satisfied that you will receive your due.

You should not be anxious to believe that there will be a reward and life, that cannot be otherwise, but be careful not to destroy this life and do not forget that it is given us that we may bring forth its fruits and fulfill the will of the Father.

Lk xii
35 - 38

So be always ready, like servants awaiting a master, to answer Him immediately he comes. The servants do not know whether he will come early or late, but they should always be ready. And if they meet their master they have fulfilled his will and it will be well for them.

So it is in life. Always, at every minute of the present, you should live the life of the spirit, not thinking of the past or the future and not saying to yourself. then or there I will do this or that.

Lk xii 39

If a master knew when a thief would come, he would not sleep, so you too should never sleep; because for the life of the son of man time is nothing; he lives only in the present and does not know when his life begins or ends.

Mt xxiv
45 - 46
Mt xxiv
48 - 51

Our life is like the life of a slave whom his master has left to manage his household. It is well for that slave if he always does his master's will. But if he says: The master will not return just yet, and neglects his business, his master will come unexpectedly and drive him out.

Mk xiii 33
Lk xxi 34

Do not be downcast, but live always in the present, by the spirit. For the life of the spirit there is no time. Look to it that you do not weigh yourself down with cares, and do not befog yourself with drunkenness or gluttony, and do not let the time for salvation pass. The time for salvation is thrown like a net over all - it is always there. Live therefore always the life of the son of man.

Mt xxv
1 - 7

We may compare the kingdom of heaven to this: Ten maidens went with lamps to meet a bridegroom. Five of them were wise and five were foolish. The foolish ones took lamps without any extra oil, but the wise ones took lamps and a supply of oil. While they waited for the bridegroom they went to sleep. When the bridegroom was approaching

Mt xxv 10

the foolish maidens saw that they had too little oil and went to buy some, but while they were gone the bridegroom came. And the wise maidens who had oil went in with him and the doors were shut. Their business was only this: to meet the bridegroom with lights. But the foolish ones had forgotten that it was important not only that the lights should burn, but that they should burn at the proper time. And in order that they should be alight when the bridegroom came, it was necessary that they should burn all the time.

Life is only for this: to exalt the son of man, and the son of man is always here, he does not belong to some particular time, and so to serve him one must live without time - in the present alone.

Therefore strive to enter into the life of the spirit now. If you do not make efforts you will not enter it. You will say: We said so and so. But there will be no good works to show, and there will be no life. For the son of man - the one true spirit of life - will appear in each man according to his deeds.

Lk xiii 24 - 25

Mt xvi 27

Mankind is divided according to the way men serve the son of man. And by their works men will be separated into two groups, as sheep from goats in a flock. The one will live, the other will perish.

Mt xxv 32

They who have served the son of man will receive what has been theirs from the beginning of the world - the life which they have preserved. They have preserved life by serving the son of man. They have fed the hungry, clothed the naked, welcomed strangers, visited those in prison. They have lived by the son of man, felt that he is the same in all men, and have therefore loved their neighbors.

Mt xxv 34

Those who have not lived by the son of man, have not served him, have not understood that he is the same in all men and have therefore not united with him, have lost the life they had in him and have perished.

IX: TEMPTATIONS

*The deceptions of temporal life hide from men
thetrue life in the present.*

"AND FORGIVE US OUR DEBTS AS WE FORGIVE OUR DEBTORS"

Mt xix
13 - 14

Lk viii 17

Mt viii 3

Mt viii 5

Lk ix 48
Mt xviii 10

Mt xviii 14
Mt xviii
6 - 8

Some children were brought to Jesus and he saw that his pupils were sending them away. He was grieved at this and said: It is wrong to send children away. They are better than anyone, for they live according to the will of the Father: they are indeed in the kingdom of heaven. Instead of sending them away you should learn from them, for to live in the Father's will you must live as children do. They do not abuse people, do not bear ill-will, do not lust, do not bind themselves by oaths, do not resist evil, do not go to law with anyone, acknowledge no difference between their own and other nations; and so they are better than grown-up people and are in the kingdom of heaven. If you do not become as children and refrain from all the snares of the flesh, you will not be in the kingdom of heaven.

Only he understands my teaching who recognizes that children are better than we, because they do not infringe the Father's will.

Only he who understands my teaching understands the will of the Father. We must not despise children. They are better than we, and their hearts are always with the Father and are pure in his sight.

Not one child perishes by the Father's will. They perish only because men entice them and draw them away from the truth. Be careful therefore not to lead a child away from the Father and from true life; for he who leads a child away from purity does evil. To lead a child away from goodness, to tempt him, is as bad as to hang a millstone about his neck and throw him into the water. It is hard for him to get out, and he is more likely to drown. Equally hard is it for a child to escape from the temptations into which a grown-up man leads him.

The world of men is unhappy only because of temptations. Temptations are everywhere in the world; they always were and always will be, and man perishes on account of them.

So give up everything, sacrifice everything, in order to avoid falling into temptation. If a fox is caught in a trap it will wrench off its paw to escape, and the paw will heal and the fox remain alive. You too should be ready to give up everything in order not to sink into temptation.

Beware of the temptation to break the first commandment: not to Lk vii 3 be angry with people when they injure you and you wish for revenge.

If a man has injured you do not forget that he is a son of the same Mt xviii Father and is your brother. If he has offended you go and appeal to his 15 - 16 conscience face to face. If he listens to you, you are a gainer and have found a new brother. If he does not listen to you, take two or three others with you to persuade him, and if he repents forgive him. Forgive Lk xvii 4 him always, even if he offends you seven times and seven times asks for forgiveness. If he will not listen to you then tell the congregation of Mt xviii 17 those who believe in my reaching, and if he will not listen to them, still forgive him, and have nothing more to do with him.

For the Kingdom of God may be compared to this: A king began to Mt xviii settle with his vassals. And they brought to him a man who owed him 23 - 35 a million and had nothing to pay with. And the king would have had to sell the vassal's land, his wife, his children, and the man himself. But the vassal begged mercy of the king, and the king had mercy on him and forgave him all his debt. Now this same man went home and saw a peasant who owed him fifty pence. And he seized the peasant and began to throttle him, and said: Pay what you owe me. And the peasant fell at his feet and said: Have patience with me and I will pay you all. But the other showed him no mercy and put him in prison, to stay there till he paid everything. Other peasants saw this and went to the king and told what the vassal had done. Then the king called the vassal and said to him: Wretched man, I forgave you all your debt because you begged me to, and you should have forgiven your debtor as I forgave you. And the king was angry and handed the vassal over to be tortured till his whole debt should be paid.

And the Father will deal with you in like manner if you do not with your whole heart forgive all those who are to blame in your sight.

You know that if you have a quarrel with a man, it is better to make Mt v 25 it up with him without going to law. You know that and act accordingly, because you know that if you go to law you will lose more. So it is with all anger. If you know that anger is an evil thing and separates you from the Father, then get rid of the anger as quickly as possible and make peace.

You know that as you become bound on earth, so will you be bound before the Father. And as you free yourselves on earth so you will also be free before the Father.

Understand that if two or three are united on earth in my teaching, Mt xviii all that they desire they already have from my Father. Because where 18 - 20 two or three are joined together in the name of the spirit in man, that spirit of man already lives in them.

Mk x 2

Beware also of temptation under the second commandment: about men changing their wives.

Mt xix
3 - 6

Some Orthodox teachers once came to Jesus, and trying him, said: May a man put away his wife?

He answered: From the very beginning man was created male and female: that was the Father's will.

Mt xix
8 - 12

Therefore a man leaves father and mother and cleaves to his wife, and the husband and wife unite in one body. So that his wife is for a man the same as his own flesh. Therefore a man must not break the natural law of God and divide what is united. In your law of Moses it is said that you may put away your wife and take another, but that is wrong. According to the Father's will it is not so. And I tell you that he who casts off his wife drives both her and him who unites with her into depravity. And by casting off his wife a man spreads dissoluteness abroad.

And his pupils said to Jesus: It is too hard to be always bound to one wife. If that must be, it would be better not to marry at all.

He said to them: You may refrain from marriage but you must understand what that means. If a man wishes to live without a wife, let him be quite pure and not approach women: but let him who loves women unite with one wife and not cast her off or look at other women.

Beware of temptation against the third commandment: about being forced to fulfill obligations as a result of taking oaths.

Mt xvii
24 - 27

The tax-collectors once came to Peter and asked him: What about your teacher - does he pay the tax? Peter said: No, he does not. And he went and told Jesus that the tax-collectors had stopped him and had said that everyone was bound to pay the taxes.

Then Jesus said to him: A king does not take taxes from his sons, nor do they have to pay them to anyone else. Is that not so? So it is with us. If we are sons of God we are bound to no one but God, and are free from all obligations. But if they demand the tax from you, then pay: not that you are under obligation to do so but because you must not resist evil. Otherwise resistance to evil will produce worse evil.

Mt xxii
16 - 21

Another time the Orthodox together with Caesar's officials went to Jesus to entrap him in his words. They said to him: You teach everyone according to the truth. Tell us, then, are we bound to pay taxes to Caesar or not? Jesus understood that they wished to convict him of not acknowledging the duty to Caesar. And he said to them: Show me what the taxes to Caesar are paid with. They handed him a coin. He looked at it and said: What is this on it? Whose is this image and inscription?

They said: Caesar's. And he said: Then give back to Caesar what is Caesar's, but that which is God's - your soul - give to no one but God. Money, property, your labor, give to him who asks them of you. But give your soul to no one but God.

You Orthodox teachers go about everywhere making people swear and vow that they will fulfill the law. But by this they only pervert people and make them worse than before. It is impossible to let the body put the soul under obligation. In your soul, God is; and you cannot make promises on God's behalf to other men. Mt xxiii 15 - 16 Mt xxiii 22

Beware of the temptation to break the fourth commandment about judging and executing people and calling on others to take part in these judgments and executions.

The pupils of Jesus once went into a village and asked for a night's lodging but were not admitted. Then they went to Jesus to complain, and said: Let lightning destroy these people! Lk ix 52 - 56

Jesus answered: You still do not understand of what spirit you are. I do not teach to destroy people but to save them.

Once a man came to Jesus and said: Bid my brother give me my inheritance. Lk xii 13 - 14

Jesus said to him: No one has made me a judge over you, and I judge no one. Neither may you sentence anyone.

The Orthodox once brought a woman to Jesus and said: See, this woman was taken in adultery. Now by the law she should be stoned to death, but what do you say about it? Jn viii 3 - 11

Jesus answered nothing, and waited for them to bethink themselves. But they pressed him, and asked him what he would adjudge to this woman? Then he said: Let him among you who has no fault cast the first stone at her. And he said nothing more.

Then the Orthodox looked within themselves and their conscience smote them, and those in front drew behind the others and they all went away.

Jesus remained alone with the woman. He looked round, saw that there was no one else, and said to her: Has no one condemned you?

She said: No one!

Then he said: Neither do I condemn you. Go, and in future do not sin.

Beware! The temptation against the fifth commandment is for men to consider it their duty to do good to their fellow-countrymen only and to regard other nations as enemies.

A teacher of the law wished to test, Jesus and said to him: What must I do to obtain life? Lk x 25

Jesus replied: You yourself know what to do: love your Father, God, and your brothers, His sons, whether they are your fellow-countrymen or not.

And the teacher of the law said: That would be well if there were not different nations, but how am I to love an enemy of my own people?

And Jesus said: There was a Jew who fell into misfortune. He was beaten, robbed, and left on the road. A Jewish priest passed by, looked at the injured man and went on. Then a Jewish Levite passed, looked at the injured man and also passed by. Then there came a man of another, a hostile nation, a Samaritan. This Samaritan saw the Jew and pitied him, not thinking of the Jews' contempt for the Samaritans. He washed and bound up his wounds, took him on his own ass to an inn, paid money for him to the innkeeper and promised to call again and pay for him.

See that you too behave like that to foreigners and to those who despise and ruin you. Then you will obtain true life.

Jesus said: The world loves its own but hates God's people. Therefore men of the world - priests, preachers, officials - will harass those who fulfill the Father's will. I am going to Jerusalem and they will torture and kill me, but my spirit cannot be killed and will remain alive.

Having heard that Jesus would be tortured and killed in Jerusalem, Peter was sad and took Jesus by the hand and said to him: If that is so, you had better not go to Jerusalem.

Then Jesus said to Peter: Do not say that. What you say is a temptation. If you fear tortures and death for me it means that you are not thinking of what is godly - of the spirit - but are thinking of what is human.

And having called the people and his pupils to him Jesus said: He that wishes to live according to my teaching let him forsake his fleshly life and be ready for all physical sufferings: he who fears for his physical life will ruin his true life, but he who disregards his fleshly life will save his true life.

But they did not understand this, and then some materialists came, and he explained to all what true life and the awakening from death means.

These materialists believed that after the death of the body there is no other life. They said: How can anybody rise from the dead? If everybody rose, they could not live together. For instance, there were seven brothers among us. The first married and died. His wife married the second brother, and he died; and she then married the third, who
also died, and so on to the seventh. Now how can those seven brothers

all live with one wife if they all rise from the dead?

Jesus answered them: Either you purposely confuse things or you do not understand what the awakening to life is. In this life people marry. But those who earn everlasting life and awaken from death do not marry and cannot die, for they are united to the Father. In your scriptures it is written that God said: I am the God of Abraham and Jacob. And this was said when Abraham and Jacob had died from among men. So those who are dead from among men are alive to God. If God is, and God does not die, then they who are with God live always. The awakening from death is to live in the will of the Father. For the Father there is no time, and therefore by fulfilling the Father's will and uniting with him man departs from time and death.

Lk xx
34 - 36

Mt xxii
31 - 32

When they heard this the Orthodox did not know what to devise to silence Jesus, and together they began to question him. And one of them said: Teacher, which in your opinion is the chief commandment of the whole law?

Mt xxii
34 - 37

They thought that Jesus would get confused in answering about the law.

But Jesus said: The chief commandment is that you should love with all your soul the Lord your God in whose power you are. And the other commandment to love your neighbor follows from it, for the same Lord God is in him also. In this is the substance of all that is written in your scriptures.

Mt xxii
37

Mt xxii
39 - 40

And he said further: What in your opinion is Christ? Is he someone's son?

Mt xxii
42 - 43

They said: In our opinion Christ is the son of David.

He replied: How then is it that David calls Christ his Lord? Christ is neither David's son, nor anyone's son after the flesh, but Christ is that same Lord, our Ruler, whom we know in ourselves as our life. Christ is that consciousness which is within us.

And Jesus said: Beware of the leaven of the Orthodox teachers. Beware also of the leaven of the materialists and of the rulers. But most of all, beware of the leaven of the self-styled 'Orthodox', for in them is the chief stumbling-block.

Lk xii 1

Lk xii 5

And when the people understood what he was speaking about, he repeated: Most of all, beware of the teaching of the scholars, the self-styled Orthodox. Beware of them, because they occupy the place of the prophets who declared the will of God to the people. They have of themselves assumed the authority to preach the will of God to the people. They preach words, but do nothing. They only say: Do this and do that.

Lk xx
45 - 46

Mt xxiii
2 - 5

But there is nothing to do, because they do nothing good, but only talk. They tell people to do what cannot be done, and they themselves do nothing. They only try to keep the teaching in their own hands, and for that purpose strive to appear imposing; they dress themselves up and exalt themselves. Know therefore that no one should call himself a teacher and leader. The self-appointed Orthodox call themselves teachers, and by so doing hinder you from entering into the kingdom of heaven, and do not enter it themselves. These Orthodox think that people can be brought to God by external ceremonies and pledges. Like blind men they do not see that the outside show is of no importance and that everything depends on the soul. They themselves do what is easy and external, but what is needful and difficult - love, mercy, and truth - they neglect. They only wish to appear to be within the law and to bring others outwardly to the law. Therefore they are like painted tombs, which seem clean externally but are loathsome within. They outwardly honor the holy martyrs, but in fact they are just the people who torture and kill the saints. They were, and are, the enemies of all that is good. All the evil in the world comes of them, because they hide the good and put forward evil in its stead. Most of all to be feared, therefore, are the self-appointed teachers. You yourselves know that every other mistake may be corrected, but if people are mistaken as to what is good it cannot be corrected, and that is the case with the self-appointed leaders.

And Jesus said: I wished here in Jerusalem to unite all men in one understanding of true happiness, but the people here are only capable of putting the teachers of goodness to death. Therefore they will remain as godless as they were, and will not know the true God till they lovingly accept the understanding of Him. And Jesus went away from the temple.

Then his pupils said to him: But what will happen to the temple of God, with all the embellishments people have brought to it to give to God?

And Jesus said: I tell you truly that this whole temple with all its embellishments will be destroyed, and nothing will be left of it. There is only one true temple of God - the hearts of men when they love one another.

And they asked him: When will that temple be?

And Jesus said to them: It will not be yet. People will for a long time be deceived in the name of my teaching, and this will cause wars and rebellions. There will be much wrong-doing and little love. But when the true teaching spreads abroad among all men, then there will be an end of evil and temptations.

Mt xxiii 8

Mt xxiii 13

Mt xxiii
15 - 16

Mt xxiii 23

Mt xxiii 28

Mt xxiii 27

Mt xxiii
30 - 31

Mk iii
28 - 29

Mt xxiii
37 - 39

Mt xxiv
1 - 4

Mt xxiv
12 & 14

X: THE STRUGGLE WITH TEMPTATION

So, not to fall into temptation, we must at every moment
Of our life be at one with the Father.

"AND LEAD US NOT INTO TEMPTATION"

After this, the Orthodox chief priests tried to do all they could to
ensnare Jesus, so as in one way or other to destroy him. They assembled
in council and began to consider.

Lk xi 53
Jn xi
47 - 48

They said: We must somehow finish with this man. He so proves his
teaching that if we let him alone everyone will believe in him and cast
off our belief. Now already half the people believe in him. But if the
Jews come to believe his teaching that all men are sons of one Father
and are brothers, and that our Hebrew people are not different from
others, then the Romans will overwhelm us completely and we shall no
longer have a Hebrew kingdom.

And the Orthodox chief priests and scholars long consulted together
and could not decide what to do with him, for they could not make up
their minds to kill him.

Lk xix
47 - 48

Then one of them, Caiaphas, who was the high priest that year, said
to them: You must remember that it is expedient to kill one man rather
than let the whole people perish, and if we leave this man alone the
people will perish. I warn you of that, so it is better to kill Jesus. Even if
the people did not perish, still they will be scattered and will go astray
from the one faith unless we kill this man. So it is better to kill him.

Jn xi
49 - 57

And when Caiaphas said this they all agreed not to hesitate, but that
it was necessary to kill Jesus without fail.

They would at once have taken him and killed him, but he withdrew
from them into the desert. But just then the feast of the Passover
occurred, when many people assembled in Jerusalem for the holiday;
and the Orthodox chief priests counted on Jesus coming with the people
to the feast. So they made known to the people that if anyone saw Jesus
he should bring him to them.

And it so happened that six days before the Passover Jesus said to
his pupils: Let us go to Jerusalem.

Jn xii 1
Jn xi
7 - 10

But the pupils said to him: Do not go. The chief priests have resolved
to stone you to death. If you go there they will kill you.

Jesus said to them: I cannot fear anything because I live in the light of understanding. And as every man, that he may not stumble, walks by day and not by night, so every man, that he may not doubt or fear, must live by this understanding. Only that man doubts and fears who lives by the flesh; he who lives by understanding neither doubts nor fears anything.

Jn xii 1 - 5

And Jesus came to the village of Bethany near Jerusalem, to the house of Martha and Mary. And when he sat at supper Martha waited on him. But Mary took a pound of fresh scented oil, poured it over his feet and wiped them with her hair.

When the scent of the oil had filled the whole room, Judas Iscariot said: Mary was wrong to waste this expensive oil; it would have been better to sell it for three hundred pence and give it to the poor.

But Jesus said: You will have the poor always with you, but I shall soon have gone away. She has done well! She has prepared my body for its burial.

Jn xii 12 - 14

In the morning Jesus went to Jerusalem where many people had come for the feast, and when they recognized Jesus they surrounded him, tore branches from the trees, and threw down their clothes on the road before him, and all shouted: He is our true King, he has taught us to know the true God.

Mt xxi 10 - 11

Jesus rode on an ass's foal, and the people ran before him and shouted. So he entered Jerusalem. And when he had ridden thus into the town all the people were excited and asked: Who is he? And those who knew him answered: Jesus, the prophet of Nazareth in Galilee.

Mk xi 15

And Jesus went into the temple and again drove out thence all the buyers and sellers.

Jn xii 19

When the Orthodox chief priests saw all this they said to each other: See what this man is doing. All the people follow him.

Mk xi 18

And they dared not take him straight from among the people, because they saw that the people were on his side, and they considered how to take him by cunning.

Jn xii 20 - 28

Meanwhile Jesus was in the temple and taught the people, among whom besides the Jews there were Greeks who were heathen. The Greeks had heard of Jesus's teaching and understood that he taught the truth not only to Hebrews but to all men; so they also wished to be his pupils and spoke about this to Philip. And Philip told it to Andrew.

These two feared to bring Jesus and the Greeks together. They feared that the people would be angry with Jesus for not making any difference between the Hebrews and other nations, and they long hesitated about telling, him. Afterwards they told him both together, and hearing that the Greeks wished to be his pupils Jesus was troubled. He knew that the people would hate him for making no difference between Hebrews and heathen, and yet he acknowledged himself to be one with the heathen.

He said: The time is come to explain what I understand by the 'son of man'. And though I perish in explaining this because I destroy the distinction between Jews and heathen, I will still speak the truth. A grain of wheat only fructifies when it itself perishes. He who loves his fleshly life loses the true life, but he who disregards the life of the flesh preserves the life everlasting. Let him who wishes to follow my teaching do as I do. And he who does as I do shall be rewarded by my Father. My soul is now troubled: shall I yield to consideration for my temporal life, or fulfill the will of the Father now at this hour? Can it be that now, when the hour in which I live has come, I shall say: Father, deliver me from that which I ought to do? I cannot say that, for I now live. Therefore I say: Father, show Thyself in me.

And Jesus said: Henceforth the present society of men is doomed to destruction. From this time that which rules this world shall be destroyed. And when the son of man is exalted above the earthly life he will unite all in one. Jn xii 31 - 32

Then the Jews said to him: We understand from the scriptures that there is an eternal Christ. How then do you say that the son of man shall be exalted? What does it mean - to exalt the son of man? Jn xii 34 - 36

To this Jesus replied: To exalt the son of man means to live by the light of understanding that is in you. To exalt the son of man above the earthly life means to believe in the light while there is light, in order to be a son of understanding.

He who believes in my teaching believes not in me but in that spirit which gave life to the world. And he who understands my teaching understands that spirit which gave life to the world. If anyone hears my words and does not fulfill them, it is not I who blame him, for I came not to accuse but to save. He who does not accept my teaching is accused, not by my teaching but by the understanding which is in himself. It is that which accuses him. I do not speak of myself, but say what my Father - the living spirit within me - suggests to me. That which I say has been told me by the spirit of understanding, and that which I teach is the true life. Jn xii 44 - 50

Having said this, Jesus went away and again hid from the chief priests. Jn xii 36

And among those who heard these words of Jesus were many powerful and wealthy people who believed his teaching but were afraid Jn xii 42 - 43 to acknowledge it to the chief priests. Not one of the chief priests acknowledged that he believed the teaching, for they were accustomed to judge by human standards and not by God's.

Mt xxvi
3 - 5

After Jesus had hidden himself, the chief priests and elders again gathered together at the palace of Caiaphas. And they began to plan how to take Jesus unknown to the people, for they were afraid to take him openly.

Mt xxvi
14 - 20

And one of the first twelve pupils of Jesus, Judas Iscariot, came to their council and said: If you want to take Jesus secretly so that the people may not see it, I will find a time when there will be few people with him, and will show you where he is and then you can take him. But what will you give me for that? They promised him thirty pieces of silver. He agreed; and from that time began to seek opportunity to lead the chief priests upon Jesus to take him.

Meanwhile Jesus withdrew from the people and only his pupils were with him. When the first feast of unleavened bread was at hand the pupils said to Jesus: Where shall we keep the Passover? And Jesus said: Go into the village, enter a house, say that you have not had time to prepare for the feast, and ask the man who lives there to admit us to celebrate the Passover.

The pupils did this: they asked a man in the village and he invited them in.

So they came and sat down to table Jesus and twelve pupils, Judas among them.

Jn xiii 11

Jesus knew that Judas Iscariot had already promised to betray him to death: but he did not accuse him and did not revenge himself, but as all his life he had taught his pupils love, so now he only reproved Judas

Mt xxvi 21
Mk xiv 18
Mt xxvi 23

lovingly. When they all twelve had sat down to table, he looked at them and said: Among you sits one who has betrayed me. Yes, he who eats and drinks with me will destroy me. And he said nothing more, so that they did not know of whom he spoke, and began to eat.

Mt xxvi
26 - 28

When they began to eat, Jesus took bread, broke it into twelve pieces, gave each of the pupils a piece, and said: Take and eat this - it is my body. And then he filled a cup with wine, handed it to the pupils and said: Drink all of you of this cup. And when they had all drunk he said: This is my blood. I shed it that people may know my will that

Lk xxii 18

they should forgive one another their sins. For I shall soon die and shall not be with you any more in this world, but shall join you only in the kingdom of heaven.

Jn xiii
4 - 7

After that, Jesus rose from table, girt himself with a towel, took a ewer of water, and began to wash the feet of all the pupils. When he came to Peter, Peter protested and said: Why should you wash my feet? Jesus said to him: It seems strange to you that I should wash your feet, but you will soon know why I do this. Though you are clean, not all of you are so: among you is my betrayer, to whom I gave bread and wine with my own hands and whose feet I wish to wash. Jn xiii 10

And when Jesus had washed the feet of all his pupils, he sat down again and said: Do you understand why I did this? I have done it that you may always do the same to one another. I, your teacher, do this that you may know how to behave with those who do you harm. If you have understood this and will do it, then you will be happy. When I said that one of you would betray me I did not speak of you all, for only one of you, whose feet I washed and who ate bread with me, will destroy me. Jn xiii 12
Jn xiii 14

Jn xiii
17 - 18

And having said this Jesus was troubled in spirit and again said: Yes, yes, one of you will betray me. Jn xiii
21 - 27

And again the pupils began to look at one another, not knowing of whom he spoke. One of them sat near Jesus, and Simon Peter made a sign to him that he should ask Jesus who the betrayer was. And he did so.

Jesus said: I will soak a bit of bread and will give it to him and he to whom I give it is my betrayer. And he gave the bread to Judas Iscariot and said to him: What you wish to do, do quickly.

And Judas understood that he must go away, and as soon as he had taken the sop he at once went out. And he could not be followed as it was night. Jn xiii
30 - 35

When Judas had gone, Jesus said: It is now clear to you what the son of man is, that in him is God, to make him as blessed as God Himself.

Children! I shall not be with you long. Do not argue over my teaching, as I said to the Orthodox, but do what I do. I give you a new commandment: as I have always and to the end loved you; do you always and to the end love one another. By that alone will you be distinguished. Seek only thus to be distinguished from other men - love one another.

And after that they went to the Mount of Olives. Mt xxvi
30 - 31

On the way there Jesus said to them: Now the time is coming when what was said in the scriptures will happen: the shepherd will be killed and the sheep will all be scattered. It will happen tonight. I shall be taken and you will all abandon me and scatter.

And Peter said to him: Though all others may be frightened and scatter, I will not deny you. I am ready to go with you to prison and to death. Mt xxvi
33 - 35

And Jesus said to him: I tell you that tonight, after I have been taken, before cock-crow, you will deny me not once but thrice.

Peter answered that he would never deny him; and all the other pupils said the same.

Lk xxii 36 - 36
Then Jesus said to them: Formerly neither I nor you lacked anything. You went without a wallet and without change of shoes, as I bade you. But now that I am considered an outlaw we can no longer do this, but must procure supplies and get knives that we may not perish uselessly.

Lk xxii 38
The pupils said: See, we have two knives - and Jesus replied: It is well.

Mt xxvi 36
Jn xviii 1
Having said this, Jesus went with the pupils to the garden of Gethsemane. And on reaching the garden he said: Wait you here, I wish to pray.

Mt xxvi 37 - 45
And coming up to Peter and the two sons of Zebedee he was sorrowful and distressed and he said to them: It is very hard for me - I am sad before my death.

Wait here, and do not be cast down as I am.

And he went off a little way, lay prone on the ground, and began to pray, saying: My Father, the spirit! Let it be not as I wish, which is that I should not die, but as you wish. Let me die. But for you, as a spirit, all is possible - grant that I may not fear death and may not be tempted by the flesh.

Then he arose, went to the pupils, and saw that they were cast down. And he said to them: How is it that you are not able for one hour to live in the spirit as I do? Exalt your spirit, so as not to yield to the temptation of the flesh. The spirit is strong, but the flesh is weak.

And again Jesus went apart from them, and again began to pray, saying: Father! If I must suffer and die, then let me die, and let Thy will be done!

Having said this, he again came to the pupils and saw that they were still more cast down and were ready to weep.

And he again went apart from them and for the third time said: Father, let Thy will be done.

Then he returned to his pupils and said to them: Now calm yourselves and be at ease, for it is now decided that I shall give myself up into the hands of worldly men.

XI: THE FAREWELL DISCOURSE

The personal life is an illusion of the flesh, an evil.
The true life is a life common to all men.

"BUT DELIVER US FROM EVIL"

And Peter said to Jesus: Where are you going? Jesus replied: You cannot come where I am going now, but later on you will go there too.

Jn xiii
36 - 38

And Peter said: Why do you think I have not the strength now to go where you are going? I would give my life for you.

Jesus said: You say you would give your life for me: see that you do not deny me thrice before cock-crow.

And he turned to the pupils and said: Do not be troubled or afraid, but believe in the true God of life, and in my teaching.

Jn xiv
1 - 28

The life of the Father is not only the life here on earth, there is another life also. If the life of the Father were only such a life as this, I would promise you that when I die I would go to Abraham's bosom and prepare a place for you there and that I would come and take you and that we should be happy together in Abraham's bosom. But I point out to you the path to another life.

Thomas said: But we do not know where you are going and so we cannot know the way. We want to know what there is after death.

Jesus said: I cannot show you what will be there; my teaching is the way and the truth and the life. It is impossible to be joined with the Father of life except through my teaching. If you fulfill my teaching you will know the Father.

Philip said: But who is the Father?

Jesus replied: The Father is He who gives life. I have fulfilled the Father's will and therefore by my life you can recognize the will of the Father.

I live in the Father and the Father lives in me. All that I say and do, I do by the will of the Father. My teaching is that I am in the Father and the Father in me. If you do not understand my teaching, yet you see me and what I do: and by this you may understand what the Father is. You know that he who follows my teaching may do the same as I, and even more, for I shall die, while he will still be alive. He who lives according to my teaching shall have all that he desires, for the son will be one with the Father. Whatever wish you may have that accords with my teaching will be fulfilled. But for that, you must love my teaching. My teaching will give you an intercessor and a comforter in my place. That comforter will be the consciousness of truth which worldly men do not understand, but you will know it in yourselves. You will never be alone, for the spirit of my teaching will be in you. I shall die and worldly men will not see me, but you will see me because my teaching lives and you will live by it. And then if my teaching is in you, you will understand that I am in the Father and the Father in me. He who fulfills my teaching will feel the Father in him and my spirit will live in him.

Then Judas (not Iscariot) said to him: But why cannot all men live by the spirit of truth?

And Jesus replied: The Father loves only him who fulfills my teaching and only in him can my spirit abide. My Father cannot love him who does not fulfill my teaching, for that teaching is not mine but the Father's. This is all I can tell you now. But my spirit, the spirit of truth which will take up its abode in you after I am gone, will reveal all things to you and you will remember and will understand much of what I have told you: so that you may always have a peaceful spirit, not the peace that worldly people seek, but such peace of mind that you will not fear anything. If you fulfill my teaching you need not regret my death. I, as the spirit of truth, will come to you and settle in your hearts together with a knowledge of the Father. If you fulfill my teaching you should rejoice, for instead of having me with you in the flesh, you will have the Father with you in your heart, and that is better for you.

Jn xv
1 - 27
My teaching is a tree of life. The Father is He who tends the tree. He prunes and cherishes those branches on which there is fruit, that they may yield more. Hold to my teaching of life and you will have more life. As a shoot lives not of itself but by being part of the tree, so you should live by my teaching. My teaching is the tree, you are the shoots. He who lives by my teaching of life will bring forth much fruit, for without my teaching there is no life. He who does not live by my teaching withers and perishes, just as dead branches are cut off and burnt.

If you live by my teaching and fulfill it you will have all you desire. For it is the will of the Father that you may live the true life and have what you desire. As my Father has given me what is good, so I give you the same. Hold on to this good. I have life because the Father loves me and I love the Father. You too should live by that same love, and if you live by it you will be blessed.

My commandment is that you love one another as I have loved you. There is no greater love than to sacrifice one's life for others as I have done.

You are my equals if you do what I have taught you. I do not consider you as slaves to whom orders are given, but as equals, for I have explained to you all that I have understood from the Father. You do not choose my teaching of your own will, you choose it because I have shown you the one truth by which you can live, and from which you will have all that you wish.

The whole teaching is - to love one another.

If the world hates you, do not be surprised: it hates my teaching. If you were at one with the world it would love you. But I have taken you out of the world, and for that it will hate you.

If they have persecuted me, they will persecute you also, and they will do all this because they do not know the true God. I explained to them, but they did not wish to hear me. They did not understand my teaching because they did not understand the Father. They saw my life and my life showed them their error, and they hated me yet more on that account.

The spirit of truth which will come to you will confirm this to you. But confirm it yourselves. I tell you this beforehand, that you may not be deceived when they persecute you. They will cast you out; they will think that by killing you they are doing what pleases God. And they will do all this because they do not understand either my teaching or the true God. I tell you this beforehand that you may not be surprised when it comes about.

Jn xvi 1 - 13

So I go now to that spirit which sent me, and now that you understand, you need not ask me where I am going to. Before this you were grieved that I did not tell you whither I go.

But I tell you truly that it is well for you that I am going. If I do not die the spirit of truth will not come to you, but if I die it will abide in you. That spirit will dwell in you, and it will be clear to you what is false, what is true, and how to make decision. The falsity is, that men do not believe in the life of the spirit: the truth is, that I am one with the Father: and the decision is, to destroy the power of bodily life.

I would say much more to you, but it is hard for you to understand. But when the spirit of truth dwells in you it will show you the whole truth because it will not tell you a new thing of its own, but what is from God; and it will show you the way in all circumstances of life. It too will be from the Father as I am from the Father and therefore it will tell you the same that I do.

Jn xvi 15 - 33

But when I, as the spirit of truth, shall be in you, you will not always know that I am there. Sometimes you will, and sometimes you will not, hear me.

And the pupils said to one another: What does this mean? He says: Sometimes you will, and sometimes you will not, hear me. What does it mean: Sometimes you will and sometimes you will not?

Jesus said to them: Do you not understand what it means - Sometimes you will, and sometimes you will not, hear me? You know how it is in the world: some are sad and grieved while others rejoice. You too will grieve, but your sorrow will be turned into joy. A woman in labor suffers torment, but when it is over she does not remember the suffering, for joy that she has brought a child into the world. So you will grieve, and will then suddenly realize my presence: the spirit of truth will enter into you and your grief will be turned into joy. Then you will ask nothing of me, because you will have all you desire. Then all that any one of you desires in the spirit he will have from his Father.

You formerly asked nothing of the spirit, but then you shall ask what you will and it will all be yours, so that your joy will be full. Now, as a man, I cannot tell you this clearly in words, but then - when as the spirit of truth I shall live in you - I will proclaim to you clearly about the Father. Then all that you ask of the Father in the name of the spirit will be given you not by me but by the Father, for He loves you for having received my teaching and understood that the spirit comes into the world from the Father and returns from the world to the Father.

Then the pupils said to Jesus: Now we understand everything and have nothing more to ask. We believe that you are from God.

And Jesus said: All that I have told you is to give you peace and confidence in my teaching. Whatever ills may befall you in the world, fear nothing: my teaching will overcome the world.

Jn xvii
1 - 3
After that Jesus raised his eyes to heaven, and said: My Father! You have given your son the freedom of life in order that he should receive the true life. Life is the knowledge of the true God of the understanding Jn xvii 6
Jn xvii 4 revealed by me. I have revealed you to men on earth. I have done what you bade me. I have shown men on earth that you exist. They were Jn xvii
6 - 11 yours before, but by your will I have revealed the truth to them and they have recognized you. They have understood that all they have, their very life, is from you alone and that I have taught them not of myself, but that I as well as they have come from you. I pray to you for those who acknowledge you. They have understood that all I have is yours and that what is yours is mine. I am no longer of this world, for I am returning to you; but they are in the world, and therefore, Father, I pray Jn xvii 15 you, preserve in them your understanding. I do not ask that you should take them from the world, but that you should deliver them from the

evil of the world and confirm them in your truth. An understanding of Jn xvii 17 - 18 you is the truth. My Father! I wish them to be as I am, to understand as I do that the true life began before the commencement of the world: that Jn xvii 21 they should all be one, as you, Father, are in me and I in you, and that they should be one with us - I in them and you in me, so that all should Jn xvii 23 be one: and that men should understand that they were not self-created, but that you have sent them into the world in love, as you sent me. Father of truth! The world did not know you, but I knew you, and men Jn xvii 25 - 26 have known you through me. I have made plain to them what you are. You are in me that the love with which you have loved me may be in them also. You have given them life, which is proof that you love them. I have taught them to know this and to love you, so that your love may return to you from them.

XII: THE VICTORY OF SPIRIT OVER MATTER

And so for a man who lives not the personal life but the
common life in the will of the Father, there is no
death. Physical death is union with the Father.

"FOR THINE IS THE KINGDOM, THE POWER, AND THE GLORY"

Mt xxvi
46 - 52

After this Jesus said: Come now, let us go: he who will betray me is near.

Hardly had he said this before Judas, one of the twelve pupils, appeared, and with him a large throng carrying sticks and swords. Judas said to them: I will show you where he is with his pupils, and that you may know him among them all, he whom I shall first kiss, is he. And he at once went up to Jesus and said: Hail, master! and kissed him.

And Jesus said to him: Why are you here, friend?

Then the guard surrounded Jesus and were about to take him.

And Peter snatched a sword from a servant of the high priest and slashed the man's ear.

But Jesus rebuked him and said: You must not resist evil. Do not do so. Give back the sword to him from whom you took it, for he who takes the sword shall perish with the sword.

Mt xxvi 55

Then he turned to the crowd and said: Why have you come out against me with weapons as if I were a robber? I was among you every

Lk xxii 53

day teaching in the temple and you did not take me. But now is your hour and the power of darkness.

Mt xxvi 56

And seeing that he was taken, the pupils all fled.

Jn xviii
12 - 14

Then the officer told the soldiers to take Jesus and bind him. They did so and took him first to Annas. This was the father-in-law of Caiaphas, who was high priest that year and lived in the same palace with Annas. He was the same Caiaphas who had planned how to destroy Jesus, saying that it was good for the people that Jesus should be killed, and that if this was not done it would be worse for the whole people. So

Mk xiv 53

Jesus was taken to the palace where this high priest lived.

Mt xxvi 58

When Jesus came there one of his pupils, Peter, followed him from afar to see where they would take him, and when Jesus was led into the court of the high priest, Peter went in also to see how the matter would

Mt xxvi
69 - 75

end. And a girl in the yard saw Peter and I said to him: You also were with Jesus of Galilee! But Peter was afraid that he might be accused, and said aloud before all the people: I do not know what you are talking about! Afterwards, when Jesus had been taken into the house, Peter also went into the passage with the people. A woman was warming herself there at the fire, and Peter went up to it. She looked at Peter and said to the others: See, this man is like one who was with Jesus of Nazareth. Peter was still more frightened, and swore that he had never been with Jesus and did not know him at all. A little later people went up to Peter and said: It is easy to see that you also were one of these disturbers. We can tell by your speech that you are from Galilee. Then Peter began to affirm and swear that he had never known or seen Jesus.

And he had hardly said this before the cock crew. And he remembered the words Jesus had said to him when he had assured Jesus that though all should abandon him he would not deny him: 'Before the cock crows this night you will deny me thrice.' And Peter went out into the yard and wept bitterly. He wept because he had fallen into temptation: he had fallen into one temptation, that of strife, when he tried to defend Jesus, and into another temptation, the fear of death, when he denied Jesus.

And the Orthodox chief priests, the scribes, and the officers, came together to the high priest. And when they were all assembled, they brought in Jesus, and the high priest asked him what his teaching was and who were his pupils.

Mk xiv 53
Jn xviii
19 - 23

And Jesus answered: I always spoke openly before all men and h id nothing, and I hide nothing from anyone. Why do you ask me? Ask those who heard and understood my teaching. They will tell you.

When Jesus said this, a servant of the high priest struck him in the face and said: To whom are you speaking? Is that the way to answer the High Priest?

Jesus said: If I have spoken ill, tell me what I have said that is wrong. But if I said nothing ill, why strike me?

The Orthodox chief priests tried to accuse Jesus, but at first found no proof on which he could be condemned. Then they found two witnesses who said of him: We ourselves heard this man say: 'I will destroy this temple of yours made with hands and in three days will build up another temple to God, not made with hands.' But this evidence also was not enough to convict him. And so the high priest called Jesus up and said: Why do you not answer their evidence?

Mt xxvi
59 - 61

Mt xxvi 59
Mt xxvi
62 - 68

Jesus remained silent.

Then the high priest said to him: Tell me, are you the Christ, a son of God?

Jesus answered him and said: Yes, I am the Christ, a son of God.

And you will yourself now see that the son of man is equal to God.

Then the high priest cried out: you blasphemer! Now we need no more evidence. We have all heard that you are a blasphemer! And the high priest turned to the assembly and said: You have yourselves heard that he blasphemes God. What do you condemn him to for that?

And they answered: We condemn him to death.

Mt xxvi 67 - 68

Then all the people and the guards fell upon Jesus and spat in his face and struck him and mishandled him. They bound his eyes, and hit him on the cheek and asked: Now, prophet, who was it that struck you?

Jesus held his peace.

Mt xxvii 2
Jn xviii 28 - 32

Having reviled him, they led him bound to Pontius Pilate and took him to the hall of judgment.

Pilate the governor came out to them and asked: Of what do you accuse this man?

They said: He is an evil doer, so we have brought him to you.

Pilate said to them: But if he does you harm, judge him yourselves according to your law.

But they replied: We have brought him to you that you may execute him, for the law does not allow us to kill anyone.

And so what Jesus had expected came to pass. He had said that he must be ready to die on the cross at the hands of the Romans instead of dying a natural death or perishing at the hands of the Jews.

Lk xxiii 2

And when Pilate asked what they accused him of, they said he was guilty of stirring up the people, forbidding them to pay tribute to Caesar, and made himself out to be the Christ and a king.

Jn xviii 33 - 38

Pilate listened to what they had to say, and then ordered Jesus to be brought to him to the judgment seat. When he came in, Pilate said: So you are king of the Jews?

Jesus replied: Do you really think I am a king, or are you only repeating what has been told you?

Pilate said: I am not a Jew so you cannot be my king, but your own people have brought you to me. What kind of a man are you?

Jesus replied: I am a king, but my kingdom is not an earthly one. If I were an earthly king my subjects would fight for me and would not have given me up to the chief priests. But, as you see, my kingdom is not an earthly one.

Pilate replied: Yet you consider yourself a king? Jesus said: Not only I, but you also, cannot but account me a king. I only teach in order to reveal to all men the truth of the kingdom of heaven. And everyone who lives by the truth is a king.

Pilate said: You speak of 'the truth' but what is truth?

And having said this he turned away and went out to the chief priests and said to them: I do not find that this man has done anything wrong.

But the chief priests insisted, and said that he did much evil and stirred up the people and had raised all Judea, right from Galilee.

Mk xv 3 - 15

Then Pilate again began to question Jesus in the presence of the chief priests, but Jesus did not answer. Pilate then said to him: Do you not hear how they accuse you? Why do you not defend yourself?

But Jesus was still silent and said not another word, so that Pilate wondered at him.

Then Pilate remembered that Galilee was under the jurisdiction of King Herod, and asked: Is he not from Galilee?

Lk xxiii 6 - 15

They told him: Yes.

Then he said: If he is from Galilee he is under Herod's authority and I will send him to him.

Herod was then in Jerusalem, and Pilate, to rid himself of Jesus, sent him to Herod.

Herod was very glad to see Jesus when they brought him. He had heard much about him and wished to know what kind of a man he was. So he called him up before him and began to question him about all he wished to know. But Jesus gave him no answer. And the chief priests and scribes accused him vehemently, as they had done before Pilate, and said that he was a rioter. And Herod regarded Jesus as an empty fellow, and to mock him had him dressed in a crimson robe, and sent him back to Pilate. Herod was pleased that Pilate had treated him with respect by sending Jesus to him to be judged, and so they were reconciled after having previously been at variance.

Now when Jesus was brought back to Pilate, Pilate again called the chief priests and rulers of the Jews and said to them. You brought this man to me for stirring up the people, and I examined him in your presence and do not find him to be a rioter. I sent him with you to Herod, and you see that again he is not convicted of any wrong-doing. I do not see any reason for condemning him to death: would it not be better to chastise him and let him go?

But when the chief priests heard this, they all cried out: No, punish him in the Roman way! Crucify him!

Mt xxvii 23

Pilate listened to the chief priests and said to them: Very well! But you have a custom at the feast of the Passover to pardon one prisoner. Well, here I have in prison Barabbas, a murderer and robber. Which of the two shall be released: Jesus or Barabbas?

Mt xxvii 21 - 23

Pilate wished thus to save Jesus, but the chief priests had so influenced the people that they all cried out: Barabbas! Barabbas!

And Pilate said: But what shall be done with Jesus?

They again cried: Crucify him in the Roman way, crucify him!

And Pilate tried to persuade them, and said: Why are you so hard on him? He has done nothing to deserve death and has done you no harm.

Jn xix 4

I will let him go, for I find no fault in him.

Jn xix 6 - 12

The chief priests and their servants cried: Crucify him! Crucify him!

And Pilate said to them: Then take him and crucify him yourselves, for I see no fault in him.

The chief priests answered: We ask only what our law demands. By our law he ought to die for making himself out to be a son of God.

When Pilate heard these words he was troubled, for he did not know what the term 'son of God' meant. And returning to the judgment hall he again called up Jesus and asked him: Who are you and where are you from?

But Jesus did not answer him.

Then Pilate said to him: Why do you not answer me? Do you not see that you are in my power and that I can crucify you or set you free?

Jesus answered him: You have no power. All power is above.

Jn xix 15

Still Pilate wished to release Jesus, and he said to the Jews: How is it that you wish to crucify your king?

Jn xix 12

But they said to him: If you release Jesus you will show yourself a disloyal servant to Caesar, for he who sets himself up as a king is

Jn xix 15

Caesar's enemy. Our king is Caesar; but let this man be crucified!

Jn xix 13

When Pilate heard these words he understood that he could not

Mt xxvii 24 - 25

refuse to execute Jesus. And he went out to the Jews, took some water, washed his hands, and said: I am not guilty of the blood of this just man.

And the people all cried: Let his blood be upon us and on our children!

Lk xxiii 23
Jn xix 13
Mt xxvii 26
Mt xxvii 28 - 29

So the chief priests prevailed. And Pilate sat on his judgment seat and ordered Jesus first to be scourged.

After the soldiers had scourged him they put a wreath on his head and a rod in his hand and threw a red cloak on him and began to mock him, bowing down before him mocking and saying: Hail, King of the Jews! And they struck him on the cheek and on the head, and spat in his face.

Jn xix 15 - 16

But the chief priests cried: Crucify him! Our king is Caesar! Crucify him!

So Pilate gave orders that he should be crucified.

They stripped Jesus of the red cloak and put on him his own clothing, and bade him carry the cross to a place called Golgotha, there to be crucified. And he carried his cross and so came to Golgotha. And there they stretched him on a cross between two other men.

When they were nailing him to the cross, Jesus said: Father, forgive them: they know not what they do.

And when Jesus was hanging on the cross the people thronged round him and railed at him. They went up, wagged their heads at him, and said: So you wished to destroy the temple of Jerusalem and rebuild it in three days! Well now, save yourself and come down from the cross! And the chief priests and leaders stood there also and mocked him, saying: He saved others, but cannot save himself".

Show us now that you are the Christ. Come down from the cross and we will believe you. He said he was the son of God and that God would not forsake him! Has not God forsaken him? And the people and the chief priests and the soldiers railed at him, and even one of the robbers crucified with him railed at him.

This robber, railing at him, said: If you are the Christ, save yourself and us!

But the other robber heard this and said: Do you not fear God? You are yourself on the cross and yet rail at an innocent man. You and I are executed for our deserts, but this man has done no harm.

And turning to Jesus he said: Lord, remember me in your kingdom!

And Jesus said to him: Even now you are blessed with me!

And at the ninth hour, Jesus, worn out, cried aloud: *Eli, Eli, lama sabaclithani*! which means: My God, my God! Why hast thou forsaken me?

And when the people heard this, they began to jeer and said: He is calling the prophet Elias! Let us see whether Elias will come!

Then Jesus said: I thirst! And a man took a sponge, dipped it in vinegar that stood by, and gave it to Jesus on a reed.

And when Jesus had sucked the sponge he cried out in a loud voice: It is finished! Father, into Thy hands I resign my spirit! And letting his head droop he gave up the ghost.

Mt xxvii 31

Jn xix 18

Lk xxiii 34 - 35

Mk xv 29 - 32

Lk xxiii 39 - 43

Mt xxvii 46 - 47

Jn xix 28

Jn xix 30
Lk xxiii 46

A Prologue

The Understanding of Life

Jesus Christ's announcement replaced the belief
in an external God by an understanding of life.

The Gospel is the revelation of this truth, that the first source of everything is the understanding of life itself. This being so, the Gospel puts in the place of what men call 'God' a right understanding of life. Without this understanding there is no life; men only live in so far as they understand life.

Those who do not grasp this, and who deem that the body is the source of life, shut themselves out from the source of true life; but those who comprehend that they live, not through the body, but through the spirit, possess true life. This is that true life that Jesus Christ came to teach to men. Having conceived that man's life flows from understanding, he gave to men the teaching and example of a life of the understanding in the body.

Earlier religions were the announcements of law as to what men ought to do, and not to do, for the service of God. The teaching of Jesus, on the other hand, deals only with the understanding of life. No man has ever seen, and no man can see or know, an external God; therefore our life cannot take for its aim the service of such a God. Only by adopting for his supreme principle the inner understanding of life, having for its source the acknowledgement of God, can man surely travel the way of life.

The announcement of welfare by Jesus Christ, the son of God. Mk i 1

The announcement of welfare consists in this, that all men who believe that they are the sons of God obtain true life. The understanding of life is at the basis and the beginning of all. The understanding of life is God. And by the announcement of Jesus it has become the basis and beginning of all things. Jn xx 21
Jn i
1 - 5

All things have come to life by understanding, and without it nothing can live. Understanding gives true life. Understanding is the light of truth, and the light shines in the darkness and the darkness cannot extinguish it.

The true light has always existed in the world and enlightens every man who is born in the world. It was in the world, and the world only lived because it had that light of understanding. Jn i
9 - 18

But the world did not retain it. He came unto his own, and his own retained him not.

Only those who understood the enlightenment were able to become like him because they believed in his reality. Those who believed that life lies in the understanding became no longer sons of the flesh, but sons of understanding.

And the understanding of life, in the person of Jesus Christ, manifested itself in the flesh, and we understood his meaning to be that the son of understanding, man in the flesh, of one nature with the Father the source of life, is such as the Father, the source of life.

The teaching of Jesus is the full and true faith, for by fulfilling the teaching of Jesus we understand a new faith instead of the former. Moses gave us a law, but we received the true faith through Jesus Christ.

No one has seen God or will ever see God, only his son, who is in the Father, has shown us the path of life.

A SUMMARY

THE UNDERSTANDING OF LIFE IS TO DO GOOD

The announcement of blessedness made by Jesus Christ is an announcement of understanding of life

The understanding of life is this : The source of life is perfect goodness, and therefore human life is perfectly good in its nature. To understand the source of life, it is necessary to believe that our spirit, the life in man, came from this source. The man, formerly not living, is summoned into life by this, his origin. This source of life appoints blessedness for man, because its own being is blessedness.

To keep in harmony with the source of his life, a man must fix himself upon the one characteristic of this source which is comprehensible to him, and which finds blessedness in doing good. Therefore man's life must be devoted to this blessedness; that is, to doing good from love. But we can find no objects of goodness other than men. All our own bodily desires are out of harmony with this principle of blessedness; and therefore they, with all the life of the body, must be surrendered to the principle of blessedness, to active love to mankind. Love to our fellow-men follows from the understanding of life revealed by Jesus Christ. The confirmations of this understanding of life are two-fold. One is, that when not accepted, the source of life seems to be an impostor, who gives to men an unsatisfied craving for life and blessedness. The other is, that man feels in his soul that love and goodness towards his fellow-men is the only true, free, eternal life.

The First Epistle of John the Divine.

This is the announcement of the understanding of life through which men have fellowship with the Father of life, and therefore have eternal life.

Jn i
1 - 7

This is an announcement of blessedness.

The understanding of life is, that God is life and blessedness, and that in life and blessedness, death and evil do not exist.

If we say that we are at one with God, while we feel we are living in evil and death, then either we are imposing upon ourselves, or we are not doing what we ought to do.

Only by living the same life as His, do we become at one with Him.

As a teacher of this life, we have Jesus Christ, the right-living. He freed us and all who will, from wrong-living.

Jn ii
1 - 6

The proof that we know the teaching of Jesus Christ is, that we carry out his commandments. Anyone who says he knows the teaching of Jesus Christ, and does not keep his commandments, is a liar, and there is no truth in him. But the man who carries out his commandments has the love of God in him. Only through love can we know that we are at one with God.

He who says he is at one with Jesus Christ, must also live as Jesus lived.

Jn ii
9 - 11

He who says of himself that he is in life and blessedness, but hates his living brother-man, is not in life and blessedness, but in death and evil; and he does not know what he is doing; he is blind, hating the life which is in himself also.

To escape this blindness, a man must remember that everything in the world, in the earthly life, is the desire of the flesh, or vanity, and that all this is not from God. And that all this passes away, perishes. And that only he who does the will of God, which is love, endures for ever.

Jn ii
15 -17

Only he who recognises that his spirit is the offspring of the Father, is united with the Father. Therefore remain in the knowledge that you are, in the spirit, sons of the Father, God, and you will have eternal life.

Jn ii
23 - 24

God gives us the opportunity of being His sons, and like Himself. So that, in this present life, we become His sons. "We do not know what we are to be, but we know that we are like Him, and that we are united with Him.

Jn iii
1 - 11

Confidence in this eternal life rids us of our mistakes, and purifies us to the Father's purity.

For whoever commits sin, violates the will of God.

Jesus Christ came to teach us the way to deliverance from sin and unity with God. Therefore those who become united with Him can no longer sin. Only that man will sin who does not know Him. But he who lives in God, acts righteously; and only he who is not united with God, does unrighteously. He who owns his origin from God, cannot do any falsehood.

Therefore men are of two classes - men of God, and men who are not of God; men who know the right and love the brethren, and men who do not know the right and do not love the brethren.

Jn iii
14 -23
For, following the teaching of Jesus Christ, we cannot refrain from loving one another. Through the teaching of Jesus Christ, we know that we have passed from death to life, because we love the brethren, and that he who does not love his brother is in death. We know that one who does not love his living brother does not love life. And he who does not love life cannot himself possess life.

By this teaching we recognise love, in the fact that life is given to us; and we know, therefore, that we also must give up our life for our brother. So that he who, himself having the means of life, sees his brother in need, and does not yield his own life for his brother's sake, - in him there is no divine love.

We must love, not by words, but by deeds, in truth. And he who so loves has a quiet heart, because he is at one with God.

If our heart is at strife in us, we subdue it to God. For God is higher than the wishes of our hearts. But if there is no strife in our hearts, then we are blessed, and that because we do all we can, the best deeds, and fulfil all that is ordained for us.

Jn iv 4
And this is ordained for us - to believe that man is the son of God, and to love our brother. Those who do this are united with God, and are risen above the world, because that which is in us is greater, of more consequence, than all the world.

Jn iv
7 - 13
Therefore let us love one another. Love is from God, and everyone who loves is the son of God, and knows God. And he who does not love, does not know God. Because God is love.

That God is love, we know because He sent into the world this Spirit, such as He Himself is, and thereby gave us life. We did not exist, and God was under no compulsion, but He gave us life and blessedness; therefore He must love us.

No man can perfectly know God. All we can know of Him is, that He had love towards us, and because of this love gave us life. And to be in fellowship with God, we must be like Him, and do as He does; we must love one another. If we love one another, God dwells in us, and we dwell in Him.

Having understood the love of God towards us, we believe that God is love, and that he who loves is united with God. And having understood this, we do not fear death, because in this world we become such as God Himself is. Our life becomes love, and is thus freed from fear and all sufferings. Jn iv 16 - 21

We love, because He loves. And we love not a God whom no one can love, because no one sees Him, but our brother-man, whom it is possible to love.

He who says he loves God, and yet hates his brother, is deceiving himself. Because, if he does not love the brother whom he sees, how, then, can he love God whom he does not see ? For it is ordained to us to love God in our brother.

To love God, is to fulfil His commandments. And these commandments are not hard for him who, recognising that his origin is from God, rises above the world. Our faith lifts us above the world. And our faith in that which Jesus, the Son of God, taught us, is true. He has taught us that he lived in the world, not merely in the way of truth, but by the power of the spirit. And that spirit is in us, and makes us strong in truth, following out the teaching. Jn v 3 - 6

If we believe in what men affirm, why, then, should we not believe in the spirit that is in ourselves ? He who believes in that spirit of life which is in us, has assurance within himself. And he who does not believe that there is a spirit from above us, from the Father, makes God a deceiver. Jn v 9 - 12

The spirit in us affirms that our life is eternal. He who knows that this spirit is the offspring of the Infinite Spirit, and becomes like Him, has eternal life. And for him who so believes, there is no difficulty left in his life, but everything he desires in the will of the Father will come to him. Jn v 14

Therefore he who believes himself to be a son of God, will not live in any deception, but is free from evil. Because he knows that this material world is an illusion, and that in man himself there is the capacity to know that which has real existence. Jn v 18 - 20

And only the Spirit, the Son, the offspring of the Father, really exists.

A RECAPITULATION

I: THE SON OF GOD

Jesus in his childhood spoke of God as his Father, There was in Judaea at that time a prophet named John, who preached the coming of God on earth. He said that if people changed their way of life, considered all men equal, and instead of injuring, helped one another, God would appear and His Kingdom would be established on earth.

Having heard this preaching, Jesus withdrew into the desert to consider the meaning of man's life and his relation to the infinite origin of all, called God. Jesus recognized as his Father that infinite source of being whom John called God.

Having stayed in the desert for some days without food, Jesus suffered hunger and thought within himself.

As a son of God Almighty I ought to be all-powerful as He is, but now that I want to eat and cannot create bread to satisfy my hunger, I see that I am not all-powerful. But to this reflection he made answer: I cannot make bread out of stones, but I can refrain from eating, and so, though I am not all-powerful in the body I am all-powerful in spirit and can quell the body. Therefore I am a son of God not through the flesh but through the spirit.

Then he said to himself: I am a son of the spirit. Let me therefore renounce the body and do away with it. But to this he replied: I am born as spirit embodied in flesh. Such is the will of my Father and I must not resist His will.

But - he went on thinking - if I can neither satisfy the needs of my body nor free myself from it, then I ought to devote myself to the body and enjoy all the pleasures it can afford me. But to this he replied: I cannot satisfy the needs of my body, and cannot rid myself of it; but my life is all-powerful in that it is the spirit of my Father. Therefore in my body I should serve the spirit, my Father, and work for Him alone.

And becoming convinced that man's true life lies only in the spirit of the Father, Jesus left the desert and began to declare this teaching to men. He said that the spirit dwelt in him, that henceforth the heavens were open and the powers of heaven brought to man, and a free and boundless life had begun for man, and that all men, however unfortunate in the body, might be happy.

II: THE SERVICE OF GOD

The Jews who considered themselves Orthodox worshipped an external God, whom they regarded as creator and ruler of the universe. According to their teaching this external God had made an agreement with them by which He had promised to help them if they would worship Him. A chief condition of this alliance was the keeping of Saturday, the Sabbath.

But Jesus said: The Sabbath is a human institution. That man should live in the spirit is more than all external ceremonies. Like all external forms of religion the keeping of the Sabbath involves a delusion. You are forbidden to do anything on the Sabbath, but good actions should always be done and if keeping the Sabbath hinders the doing of a good action then the keeping of the Sabbath is an error.

According to the Orthodox Jews another condition of the agreement with God was avoidance of intercourse with unbelievers.

Of this Jesus said that God desires not sacrifice to Himself, but that men should love one another.

Yet another condition of the agreement related to rules for washing and purifying, as to which Jesus said that what God demands is not external cleanliness, but pity and love towards man. He also said that external rules are harmful, and that the church tradition is itself an evil. Their church tradition set aside the most important things, such as love for one's mother and father - and justified this by its traditional railings.

Of all the external regulations of the old law defining the cases in which a man was considered to have defiled himself, Jesus said: Know all of you, that nothing from outside can defile a man, only what he thinks and does can defile him.

After this Jesus went to Jerusalem, the city considered holy, and entered into the temple where the Orthodox considered that God Himself dwelt, and there he said that it was useless to offer God sacrifices, that man is more important than a temple, and that our only duty is to love our neighbor and help him.

Furthermore Jesus taught that it is not necessary to worship God in any particular place, but to serve the Father in spirit and in deed. The spirit cannot be seen or shown. The spirit is man's consciousness of his sonship to the Infinite Spirit. No temple is necessary. The true temple is the society of men united in love. He said that all external worship of God is not only false and injurious when it conduces to wrong-doing - like the Jew's worship which prescribed killing as a punishment - and allowed the neglect of parents - but also because a man performing external rites accounts himself righteous and free from the need of doing what love demands. He said that only he seeks what is good and does good deeds, who feels his own imperfections. To do good deeds a man must be conscious of his own faults, but external worship leads to a false self-satisfaction. All external worship is unnecessary, and should be thrown aside. Deeds of love are incompatible with ceremonial performances, and good cannot be done in that way. Man is a spiritual son of God and should therefore serve the Father in spirit.

III: LIFE IN THE SPIRIT

John's pupils asked Jesus what he meant by his 'kingdom of heaven' and he answered them: The heaven I preach is the same as that preached by John - that all men, however poor, may be happy.

And Jesus said to the people: John is the first prophet to preach to men a Kingdom of God which is not of the external world, but in the soul of man. The Orthodox went to hear John, but understood nothing because they know only what they have themselves invented about an external God; they teach their inventions and are astonished that no one pays heed to them. But John preached the truth of the Kingdom of God within us, and therefore he did more than anybody before him. By his teaching the law and the prophets, and all external forms of worship, are superseded. Since he taught, it has been made clear that the Kingdom of God is in man's soul.

The beginning and the end of everything is the soul of man. Every man, though he realizes that he was conceived by a bodily father in his mother's womb, is conscious also that he has within him a spirit that is free, intelligent, and independent of the body.

That eternal spirit proceeding from the infinite, is the origin of all and is what we call God. We know Him only as we recognize Him within ourselves. That spirit is the source of our life; we must rank it above everything and by it we must live. By making it the basis of our life we obtain true and everlasting life. The Father-spirit who has given that spirit to man cannot have sent it to deceive men - that while conscious of everlasting life in themselves they should lose it. This infinite spirit in man must have been given that through him men should have an infinite life. Therefore the man who conceives of this spirit as his life has infinite life, while a man who does not so conceive it has no true life. Men can themselves choose life or death: life in the spirit, or death in the flesh. The life of the spirit is goodness and light: the life of the flesh is evil and darkness. To believe in the spirit. means to do good deeds; to disbelieve means to do evil. Goodness is life, evil is death. God - an external creator, the beginning of all beginnings - we do not know. Our conception of Him can only be this: that He has sown the spirit in men as a sower sows his seed, everywhere, not discriminating as to what part of the field; and the seed that falls on good ground grows, but what falls on sterile ground perishes. The spirit alone gives life to men, and it depends on them to preserve it or lose it. For the spirit, evil does not exist. Evil is an illusion of life. There is only that which lives and that which does not live.

Thus the world presents itself to all men, and each man has a consciousness of the kingdom of heaven in his soul. Each one can of his own free will enter that kingdom or not. To enter it he must believe in the life of the spirit, for he who believes in that life has everlasting life.

IV: THE KINGDOM OF GOD

Jesus was sorry for people because they did not know true happiness, therefore he taught them. He said: Blessed are they who have no property or fame and do not care for them, and unhappy are they who seek riches and fame; for the destitute and the oppressed are in the Father's will, but the rich and famous seek only rewards from men in this temporal life.

To fulfill the will of the Father do not fear to be poor and despised, but rejoice that you can show men what true happiness is.

To carry out the will of the Father which gives life and welfare to all men, five commandments must be obeyed:

The first commandment is to do no ill to anyone so as not to arouse anger, for evil begets evil.

The second commandment is not to go after women and not to desert the wife with whom you have once been joined; for desertion and change of wives causes all the world's dissoluteness.

The third commandment is to take no oath of any kind. A man can promise nothing, for he is altogether in the Father's power; and oaths are taken for bad purposes.

The fourth commandment is not to resist evil, not to condemn, and not to go to law; but to endure wrong and to do even more than people demand, for every man is full of faults and incapable of guiding others. By taking revenge, we only teach others to do the same.

The fifth commandment is not to discriminate between fellow-countrymen and foreigners, for all are children of one Father.

These five commandments should be observed not to win praise from men, but for your own welfare; therefore do not pray, or fast, in the sight of men.

The Father knows all that people need, and there is no need to pray for anything; all that is necessary is to seek to be in the Father's will. And His will is that we should not feel enmity towards anyone. It is unnecessary to fast, for men fast merely to win praise from men and their praise should be avoided. It is necessary only to take care to live in the Father's will, and the rest will all be added of itself. A man concerned with the things of the body cannot be concerned with the kingdom of heaven. Even though a man does not trouble about food and clothing, he can live: the Father will give life. All that is needful is to be in the will of the Father at the present moment, for the Father gives his children what they need. Desire only the power of the spirit, which the Father gives. The five commandments show the path to the kingdom of heaven, and this narrow path alone leads to everlasting life.

False teachers - wolves pretending to be sheep always try to lead people astray from this path. Beware of them! False teachers can always be detected by the fact that they teach evil in the name of good. If they teach violence and executions they are false teachers. By what they teach they may be known.

Not he fulfils the Father's will who calls on the name of God, but he who does what is good. He who fulfills these five commandments will have a secure and true life, of which nothing can deprive him: but he who does not fulfill them will have an insecure life which will soon be taken from him, leaving him nothing.

The teaching of' Jesus surprised and attracted the people by the fact that it recognized all men as free. It was the fulfillment of Isaiah's prophecy, that God's chosen one would bring light to men, would overcome evil and re-establish truth, not by violence but by gentleness, meekness, and kindness.

V: THE TRUE LIFE

Wisdom lies in recognizing life as the offspring of the Father's spirit. People set themselves the aims of the bodily life, and in seeking these aims torment themselves and others. But they will find full satisfaction in the life meant for them - the life of the spirit - if they accept the doctrine of the spiritual life and of subduing and controlling the body.

It happened once that Jesus asked a woman of another religion to give him some water to drink. She refused on the plea that she was of a different faith. Jesus then said to her: If you understood that he who is asking for water is a living man in whom the spirit of the Father lives, you would not refuse him, but by doing a kindness would try to unite yourself in spirit with the Father, and that spirit would give you not such water as this - after drinking which a man thirsts again - but water that gives everlasting life. One need not pray to God in any special place, but should serve Him, by deeds of love - by ministering to those in whom His spirit dwells.

And Jesus said to his pupils: The true food of man is to fulfill the will of the Father-spirit, and this fulfillment is always possible. Our whole life is a gathering up of the fruits of the spirit sown within us by the Father. Those fruits are the good we do to men. We should do good to men unceasingly and expect no reward.

After this Jesus happened to be in Jerusalem and came to a bathing-place beside which lay a sick man, waiting for a miracle to cure him. Jesus said this to him: Do not expect to be cured by a miracle, but live according to your strength and do not mistake the meaning of life. The invalid obeyed Jesus, got up, and went away. Seeing this, the Orthodox began to reproach Jesus for having cured an invalid on the Sabbath. Jesus said to them: I have done nothing new. I have only done what our common Father-spirit does. He lives and gives life to men, and I have done likewise. To do this is every man's business. Everyone has freedom to choose life or reject it. To choose life is to fulfill the will of the Father by doing good to others; to reject it is to do one's own will and not do good to others. It is in each one's power to do the one or the other: to receive life or destroy it.

The true life of man can be compared to this: A master apportioned to his slaves a valuable property and told them each to work on what was given him. Some of them worked, others simply put away what had been given them. Then the master demanded an account of what they had done, and to those who had worked he gave still more of his property, while from those who had not worked he took away all that they had.

The portion of the master's valuable property is the spirit of life in man, who is the son of the Father spirit. He who in this life works for the sake of the spirit-life receives infinite life, he who does not work loses what was given him.

The only true life is the life common to all, and not the life of the individual. Each should work for the life of others.

After that Jesus went to a desert place and many people followed him. Towards evening his pupils came and said: How can we feed all these people?

Among the gathering were some who had no food, and some who had bread and fish. Jesus said to his pupils: Give me what bread you have. And he took the loaves and gave the bread to his pupils, and they gave it away to others, who began to do the same. So everyone ate what was distributed in this way, and they all had enough without eating all the food that was there. And Jesus said: That is how you should always act. It is not necessary for each man to obtain food for himself but it is needful to do what the spirit in man demands, namely to share what there is with others.

The true food of man is the spirit of the Father. Man lives only by the spirit.

We must serve all that has life, for life lies not in doing one's own will but the will of the Father of life. And that will is that the life of the spirit, which each one has, should remain in him and that all should cherish the life of the spirit in them until the hour of death. The Father, the source of all life, is the spirit. Life consists only in carrying out the will of the Father, and to carry out that will of the spirit one must surrender the body. The body is food for the life of the spirit.

Only by sacrificing the body does the spirit live.

After this Jesus chose certain pupils and sent them about to preach the doctrine of the life of the spirit. When sending them he said: You are going to preach the life of the spirit, therefore renounce in advance all fleshly desires and have nothing of your own. Be prepared for persecution, privation, and suffering. Those who love the life of the body will hate you, torment you, and kill you; but do not be afraid. If you fulfill the will of the Father you possess the life of the spirit, of which no one can deprive you.

The pupils set out and when they returned they announced that they had everywhere overcome the teaching of evil.

Then the Orthodox said to Jesus that his teaching, even if it overcame evil, was itself an evil, for those who carry it out must endure sufferings. To this Jesus said: Evil cannot overcome evil. Evil can only be mastered by goodness, and that goodness is the will of the Father-spirit, common to all men. Every man knows what is good for himself, and if he does that for others - if he does that which is the will of the Father - he will do good. And so the carrying out of the will of the Father-spirit is good even if it be accompanied by the suffering and death of those who fulfill that will.

VI: THE FALSE LIFE

Jesus said that his mother and his brothers had no prior claim on him as such, only those were near to him who fulfilled the will of their common Father.

A man's life and blessedness depend not on family relationships, but on the life of the spirit. Jesus said: Blessed are those who retain their understanding of the Father. A man living in the spirit has no home - the spirit cannot own a house. He said that he himself had no fixed abode. To fulfill the Father's will no special place is needed, for it is always and everywhere possible.

The death of the body cannot be dreadful to a man who resigns himself to the will of the Father, for the life of the spirit does not depend on that of the body. Jesus says that he who believes in the life of the spirit can fear nothing.

No cares make it impossible for a man to live in the spirit. To one who said that he would obey the teaching of Jesus later, but must first bury his father, Jesus replied: Only the dead trouble about the burial of the dead, the living live always by fulfilling the will of the Father.

Family and household cares must not hinder the life of the spirit. He who is troubled about what results to his bodily life from the fulfillment of the Father's will, acts like a ploughman who looks back while ploughing, instead of in front of him.

Cares for the pleasure of the bodily life, which seem so important to men, are delusions. The only real business of life is the announcement of the Father's will, attention to it, and fulfillment of it. When Martha complained that she alone busied herself about the supper, while her sister Mary listened to his teaching instead of helping, Jesus replied: You blame her unjustly. If you need the results of your work, busy yourself with it, but let those who do not need physical pleasures attend to the one thing essential for life.

Jesus said: He who desires to obtain true life, consisting in the fulfillment of the Father's will, must first of all give up his own personal desires. He must not only not plan his life according to his own wishes, but must be ready to endure privation and suffering at any moment.

He who desires to arrange his bodily life according to his own desires, will wreck the true life of fulfillment of the Father's will. And there is no advantage in gain for the physical life if that gain wrecks the life of the spirit.

Most ruinous of all for the ills of the spirit is the love of gain, of getting rich. Men forget that whatever riches or goods they obtain, they may die at any moment, and that property is not essential for life. Death hangs over each of us. Sickness, murder, or accident may at any moment end our life. Bodily death is an inescapable condition of every second of our life. While a man lives he should regard every hour of life as a postponement of death granted by someone's kindness. We should remember this, and not say we do not know it. We know and foresee all that happens on earth and in the sky, but forget death, which we know awaits us at any moment. Unless we forget death we cannot yield ourselves to the life of the body; for we cannot reckon on it. To follow the teaching of Christ we must count up the advantages of following our own will and serving the bodily life, and the advantages of fulfilling the Father's will. Only he who has clearly taken account of this can be a disciple of Christ. But he who makes the calculation will not regret having to forgo this unreal happiness and unreal life in order to obtain the true good and the true life. True life is given to men and they know it and hear its call, but constantly distracted by the cares of the moment they deprive themselves of it. True life is like a feast a rich man gave, and to which he invited guests. He called them - just as the voice of the Father-spirit calls all men to Himself. But some of those invited were busy with trading, others with their farms, others again with family affairs, and they did not go to the feast. Only the poor who had no worldly cares went to the feast and gained happiness. So men distracted by cares for the bodily life deprive themselves of true life. He who does not wholly reject the cares and gains of the bodily life cannot fulfill the Father's will, for no man can serve himself a little and the Father a little: he has to consider whether it is better to serve his body and whether it is possible to arrange his life according to his own will. He must do as a man does who wishes to build a house, or to prepare for war. That man first considers whether he has means to finish his house, or to conquer his enemy. And if he sees that he has not, he will not waste his labor or his army uselessly, and make himself a laughing-stock to his neighbors. If a man could arrange his bodily life to his own will, then it might be well to serve the body, but as that is impossible, it is better to reject bodily things and serve the spirit. Otherwise you will gain neither the one thing nor the other. You will not arrange the bodily life satisfactorily, and will lose the life of the spirit. Therefore to fulfill the Father's will it is necessary to sacrifice the bodily life.

The bodily life is wealth entrusted to us by another, which we should use so as to gain our own true riches.

If a rich man has a manager who knows that however well he may serve his master, that master will dismiss him leaving him with nothing, the manager will be wise if while managing his master's affairs he does favors to other people. Then when the master dismisses him, those whom he has benefited will receive him and sustain him. That is how men deal in their bodily life. The bodily life is that wealth, not our own, which is entrusted to us for a time. If we make good use of that wealth which is not our own, then we shall receive true wealth which will be our own.

If we do not give up wealth that is not our own, we shall not receive our true wealth. We cannot serve both the illusory life of the body and the life of the spirit; we must serve the one or the other. A man cannot serve property and God. What is honorable among men is an abomination before God. In God's sight riches are evil. A rich man is guilty in that he eats much and luxuriously, while at his door the poor are hungry. And everyone knows that property not shared with others is held in non-fulfillment of the Father's will.

A rich, Orthodox ruler came once to Jesus and began to boast that he fulfilled all the commandments of the law. Jesus reminded him that there is a commandment to love others as oneself and that that is the Father's will. The ruler said he kept that also. Then Jesus said to him: That is not true; if you really wished to fulfill the Father's will you would not possess property. You cannot fulfill the Father's will if you have property of your own which you do not give to others. And Jesus said to his pupils: Men think it impossible to live without property, but I tell you that true life consists in giving what you have to others.

A certain man named Zaccheus heard the teaching of Jesus and believed it, and having invited Jesus to his house said to him: I am giving half my fortune to the poor and will restore fourfold to those I have wronged. And Jesus said: Here is a man who fulfills the Father's will, for a man's whole life must be passed in fulfillment of that will, and there is no condition in which a man can say: 'I have fulfilled the will of God.'

Good cannot be measured; it is impossible to say who has done more or less. A widow who gives away her last farthing gives more than a rich man who gives thousands. Nor can goodness be measured by its usefulness.

Let the case of the woman who felt pity for Jesus and recklessly poured over his feet many pounds' worth of costly oil serve as an example. Judas said she had acted foolishly because the cost of the oil would have sufficed to feed many people. But Judas was a thief and a liar, and when he spoke of the material advantage he was not thinking of the poor. The essential thing lies not in the utility of an action or the largeness of a gift, but what is necessary is always, every moment, to love others and give them what one has.

VII: I AND THE FATHER ARE ONE

Answering the Jews' demand for proofs of the truth of his teaching, Jesus said: The truth of my teaching lies in the fact that I teach not something of my own but what comes from the common Father of us all. I teach what is good for the Father of all and is therefore good for all men.

Do what I say, fulfill the five commandments, and you will see that what I say is true. Fulfillment of these five commandments will drive away all evil from the world, and therefore they are certainly true. It is clear that he who teaches the will of Him who sent him, and not his own will, teaches the truth. The law of Moses teaches the fulfillment of human desires and so it is full of contradictions; my teaching is to fulfill the will of the Father and so it is harmonious.

The Jews did not understand him and looked for external proofs of whether he was the Christ mentioned in the prophecies. On this he said to them: Do not question who I am and whether it is of me that your prophecies speak, but attend to my teaching and to what I say about our common Father.

You need not believe in me as a man, but you should believe what I tell you in the name of the common Father of us all.

It is not necessary to inquire about external matters as to where I come from, but it is necessary to follow my teaching. He who follows it will receive true life. There can be no proofs of the truth of my teaching. It is the light itself, and as light cannot be illuminated, so truth cannot be proven true. My teaching is the light. He who sees it has light and life and needs no proofs, but he who is in darkness must come to the light.

But the Jews again asked him who he was as to his bodily personality. He said to them: I am, as I told you from the first, a man, the son of the Father of life. Only he who so regards himself (this is the truth I teach) will fulfill the will of the common Father; only he will cease to be a slave and become a free man. We are enslaved only by the error of taking the life of the body to be the true life. He who understands the truth - that life consists only in the fulfillment of the Father's will - becomes free and immortal. As a slave does not always remain in the house of his master, but the son does; so a man who lives as a slave to the flesh does not remain alive for ever, but he who fulfills in his soul the Father's will has eternal life. To understand me you must understand that my Father is not the same as your father whom you call God. Your father is a god of the flesh, but my Father is the spirit of life. Your father, your god, is a jealous god, a man-slayer, one who executes men. My Father gives life, and so we are the children of different fathers. I seek the truth, and you wish to kill me for that, to please your god. Your god is the devil, the source of evil, and in serving him you serve the devil. My teaching is that we are sons of the Father of life, and he who believes in my teaching shall not see death. The Jews asked: How can it be that a man will not die, when all those who pleased God most - even Abraham - have died? How then can you say that you, and those who believe in your teaching, will not die?

To this Jesus replied: I speak not by my own authority. I speak of that same source of life that you call God, and that dwells in men. That source I know and cannot help knowing, and I know His will and fulfill it, and of that source of life I say that it has been, is, and will be, and that for it there is no death.

Demands for proofs of the truth of my teaching are as if one demanded from a man who had been born blind, proofs of why and how he sees the light when his sight has been restored.

The blind man whose sight has been restored, remaining the same man he was, can only say that he was blind but now sees. And one who formerly did not understand the meaning of life but now does understand it, can only say the same, and nothing else.

Such a man can only say that formerly he did not know the true good in life but now he knows it. A blind man whose sight has been restored, if told that he has not been cured in a proper manner and that he who restored his sight is an evil-doer, and that he should be cured differently, can only reply: I know nothing about the correctness of my cure or the sinfulness of him who cured me, or of a better way of being cured; I only know that whereas I was blind, now I see. And in the same way one who has understood the meaning of the teaching of true welfare and of the fulfillment of the Father's will, can say nothing as to the regularity of that teaching or whether he who disclosed it to him was a sinner, or of the possibility of a still greater blessedness, but can only say: Formerly I did not see the meaning of life, but now I see it and that is all I know.

And Jesus said: My teaching is the awakening of a life till then asleep: he who believes my teaching awakens to eternal life and lives after death.

My teaching is not proven in any way: men yield to it because it alone has the promise of life for all men.

As sheep follow the shepherd who gives them food and guards their life, so men accept my teaching because it gives life to all. And as the sheep do not follow a thief who climbs over into the fold, but shy away from him, so men cannot believe these doctrines which teach violence and executions. My teaching is as a door for the sheep, and all who follow me shall find true life. As only those shepherds are good who own and love the sheep and devote their lives to them, while hirelings who do not love the sheep are bad shepherds, so also only that teacher is true who does not spare himself, and he is worthless who cares only for himself. My teaching is that a man should not spare himself, but should sacrifice the life of the body for the life of the spirit. This I teach and fulfill.

The Jews still did not understand and still wanted proofs of whether or not Jesus was the Christ, and whether, therefore, they should believe him or not. They said: Do not torment us, but tell us plainly, are you the Christ or not? And to this Jesus replied: Belief must be given not to words but to deeds. By the example I set, you may know whether I teach the truth or not. Do what I do, and do not discuss words. Fulfill the will of the Father, and then you will all be united with me and with the Father; for I, the son of man, am the same as the Father and the same that you call God and that I call the Father. I and the Father are one. Even in your own scriptures it is said that God said to men: 'You are Gods.' Every man by his spirit is a son of this Father. And if a man lives fulfilling the Father's will he becomes one with the Father. If I fulfill His will, the Father is in me and I am in the Father.

After this Jesus asked his pupils how they understood his teaching about the son of man. Simon Peter answered him: Your teaching is that you are the son of the God of life, and God is the life of the spirit in man. And Jesus said to him: You are happy, Simon, to have understood that. Man could not have disclosed it to you, but you have understood it because the God in you has revealed it to you. On this understanding the true life of men is founded. For that life there is no death.

VIII: LIFE IS NOT TEMPORAL

In reply to doubts expressed by his pupils as to the reward resulting for renouncing the life of the flesh, Jesus said: For him who understands the meaning of my teaching there can be no question of a reward, first because a man who for its sake gives up family, friends, and possessions, gains a hundredfold more friends and more possessions, and secondly, because a man who seeks a reward seeks to have more than others have, and that is quite contrary to the fulfillment of the Father's will. In the kingdom of heaven there is neither greater nor less, all are equal. Those who seek a reward for goodness are like laborers who, because in their opinion they were more deserving than others, demanded larger pay than they had agreed upon with their employer. According to the teaching of Jesus no one can be either higher or more important than another.

All can fulfill the Father's will, but in doing so no one becomes superior or more important or better than another. Only kings and those who serve them reckon in that way. According to my teaching, said Jesus, there can be no superior rank; he who wishes to be better should be the servant of all. My teaching is, that life is given to man not that others may serve him, but that he should give his whole life to the service of others. He who exalts himself instead of doing this, will fall lower than he was.

The meaning and purpose of life must be understood before a man can be rid of thoughts of his own elevation. The meaning of life lies in fulfilling the will of the Father, and His will is that what He has given us shall be returned to Him. As a shepherd leaves his whole flock and goes to seek a lost sheep, and as a woman will search everywhere to find a lost penny, so the Father's continual work is manifested to us by the fact that He draws to Himself that which pertains to Him.

We must understand wherein true life consists. True life always appears in the lost being restored to where it belongs, and in the awakening of those that sleep. People who have the true life and have returned to the source of their being, cannot, like worldly men, account others as being better or worse, but being sharers of the Father's life can only rejoice at the return of the lost to the Father. If a son who has gone astray repents and returns to the father he had left, how can other sons of the same father be envious of his joy, or fail to rejoice at their brother's return?

To believe in the teaching and to change our way of life and fulfill that teaching, what is needed is not external proofs or promises of rewards, but a clear understanding of what true life is. If men think themselves completely masters of their own lives, and believe that life is given them for bodily enjoyment, then clearly any sacrifice they make for others will seem to them an act worthy of reward, and without such reward they will give nothing. If tenants forgot that a garden was let to them on condition that they returned the fruits to the owner, and that rent was demanded of them again and again, they would seek to kill the collector. So it is with those who think themselves masters of their own lives and do not understand that life is granted them by an understanding which demands the fulfillment of its will. To believe and to act, it is necessary to understand that man can do nothing of himself, and that if he gives up his bodily life to serve goodness he does nothing that deserves either thanks or reward. We must understand that in doing good a man only does his duty and what he necessarily must do. Only when he understands life in that way can a man have faith enabling him to do truly good deeds.

The kingdom of heaven consists in that understanding of life. It is not a visible kingdom that can be pointed out in this or that place. The kingdom of heaven is in man's understanding. The whole world lives as of old: men eat and drink, marry, trade, and die, and along with this in the souls of men lives the kingdom of heaven - an understanding of life growing as a tree that in spring puts out leaves of itself.

True life is the fulfillment of the will of the Father, not in the past or in the future, but now; it is what each of us must do at the present moment. And therefore to live the true life we must never relax. Men are set to guard life, not in the past or in the future, but the life now being lived, and in it to fulfill the will of the Father of all men. If they let this life escape them by not fulfilling the Father's will, they will not receive it back again. A watchman set to watch all night does not perform his duty if he falls asleep even for a moment, for a thief may come at that moment. So man should direct his whole strength to the present hour, for only then can he fulfill the Father's will; and that will is the life and blessing of all men. Only those live who are doing good. Good done to men now in the present, is the life that unites us with the common Father.

IX: TEMPTATIONS

Man is born with a knowledge of the true life which lies in the fulfillment of the Father's will. Children live by that knowledge: in them the will of the Father is seen. To understand the teaching of Jesus one must understand the life of children and be like them.

Children live in the Father's will, not infringing the five commandments, and they would never infringe them were they not misled by adults. Men ruin children by leading them to break these commandments. And by so doing they act as if they tied a millstone to a man's neck and threw him into the river. The world is unhappy only because people yield to temptations, but for that the world would be happy. Temptations lure men to do evil for the sake of imaginary advantages in their temporal life. Yielding to temptation ruins men, and therefore everything should be sacrificed rather than fall into temptation.

The temptation to infringe the first commandment comes from men considering themselves in the right towards others, and others in the wrong towards themselves. To avoid falling into that temptation we must remember that all men are always infinitely in debt to the Father and can only acquit themselves of that debt by forgiving their brother men.

Therefore men must forgive injuries, and not be deterred though the offender injures them again and again. However often a man may be wronged he must forgive, not remembering the wrong; for only by forgiveness can the kingdom of heaven be attained. If we do not forgive others, we act as a certain debtor did when, heavily in debt, he went to his creditor and begged for mercy. His creditor forgave him everything, but the debtor went away and meeting a man who owed him only a small sum, began to throttle him. To have life we must fulfill the Father's will. We ask forgiveness of Him for failing to fulfill His will, and hope to be forgiven. What then are we doing if we do not ourselves forgive others? We are doing to them what we dread for ourselves.

The will of the Father is well-being; and evil is that which separates us from the Father. How then can we fail to seek to quench evil as quickly as possible, since it is that which ruins us and robs us of life? Evil entangles us in bodily destruction. In so far as we escape from that entanglement we obtain life and have all that we can desire. We are not separated from one another by evil but are united by love.

Men are tempted to infringe the second commandment by thinking of woman as created for bodily pleasure, and by supposing that by leaving one wife and taking another they will obtain more pleasure. To avoid falling into this temptation we must remember that the Father's will is, not that man should delight himself with woman's charms, but that each man having chosen a wife should be one with her. The Father's will is for each man to have one wife and each wife one husband. If each man keeps to one wife, each man will have a wife and each woman a husband. He who changes his wife deprives her of a husband and gives occasion for some other man to leave his wife and take the deserted one. A man need not marry at all, but must not have more than one wife, for if he does he goes against the will of the Father which is that one man should unite with one woman.

Men are tempted to infringe the third commandment by creating, for the advantage of their temporal life, established authorities, and demanding from one another oaths by which they bind themselves to do what those authorities demand. To avoid falling into this temptation men must remember that they are indebted for their life to no power but God. The demands of authorities should be regarded as violence but, following the command of non-resistance to evil, men should yield what goods and labor the authorities may demand. But they must not pledge their conduct by taking oaths, for the oaths that are imposed lead to evil. He who recognizes his life as being in the will of the Father cannot bind his actions by pledges, for such a man holds his life most sacred.

Men are tempted to infringe the fourth commandment by thinking that they can reform others by themselves yielding to anger and revenge. If a man wrongs another, people think he should be punished and that justice lies in human judgment.

To avoid falling into this temptation we must remember that men are called not to judge but to save one another, and that they cannot judge one another's faults because they are themselves full of wickedness. The one thing they can do is to teach others by an example of purity, forgiveness, and love.

Men are tempted to infringe the fifth commandment by thinking that there is a difference between their own countrymen and those of other nations, and that it is therefore necessary to defend themselves against other nations and do them harm. To avoid falling into this temptation it is necessary to know that all the commandments may be summed up in this: to do good to all men without distinction, and thus fulfill the will of the Father who has given life and well-being to all. Even if others make such distinctions, and though nations, considering themselves alien to one another, go to war, yet each man, to fulfill the will of the Father, should do good to all - even to those belonging to a nation with which his country is at war.

To avoid falling into human illusions we must think not of the physical but the spiritual life. If a man understands that life consists solely in now being in the Father's will, neither privations, nor sufferings, nor death, can seem dreadful to him. Only that man receives true life who is ready at every moment to give up his physical life in order to fulfill the Father's will.

And that everyone may understand that true life is that in which there is no death, Jesus said: Eternal life should not be understood as being like the present life. For true life in the will of the Father there is neither space nor time.

Those who are awake to the true life live in the Father's will for which there is neither space nor time. They live with the Father. If they have died for us, they live for God. Therefore one commandment includes in itself all: to love all men, each of whom has the source of life within him.

And Jesus said: That source of life is the Christ you are awaiting. The comprehension of that source of life, for whom there is no distinction of persons and no time or place, is the son of man whom I teach. All that hides that source of life, from men is temptation. There is the temptation of the scribes, of the bookmen, and of the materialists - do not yield to it. There is the temptation of authority, do not yield to that: and there is also the most terrible temptation, from the religious teachers who call themselves Orthodox. Beware of this last temptation more than of all the others, because these self-ordained teachers, just they, by devising the worship of a false God decoy you from the true God. Instead of serving the Father of life by deeds, they substitute words, and teach words while they themselves do nothing. You can learn nothing from them but words, and the Father requires deed. They can teach nothing because they themselves know nothing, and only for their own advantage wish to set themselves up as teachers. But you know that no man can be the teacher of another. There is one teacher for all men - the Lord of life - understanding. But these self-styled teachers, thinking to teach others, deprive themselves of true life and hinder others from understanding it. They teach men that their God will be pleased by external rites, and think they can bring men to religion by vows. They are only concerned about externals. An outward assumption of religion satisfies them, but they do not think of what goes on in men's hearts. And so they are like showy sepulchers, handsome outside but loathsome within. In words they honor the saints and the martyrs, but they are just the people who formerly killed and tortured and who now kill and torture the saints. From them come all the world's temptations for under the guise of good they teach evil.

The evil they create is the root of all others, for they defile the most holy thing in the world. They will continue their deceptions and increase evil in the world, and it will be long before they are changed. But a time will come when all their churches and all external worship of God will be destroyed, and men will understand, and unite in love, to serve the one God of life and to fulfill His will.

X: THE STRUGGLE WITH TEMPTATIONS

The Jews saw that the teaching of Jesus would destroy their State religion and their nationality, and at the same time saw that they could not refute it, so they decided to kill him. His innocence and rectitude hindered them but the high priest Caiaphas devised a pretext for killing him even though Jesus was not guilty in any way. Caiaphas said: We need not discuss whether this man is innocent or guilty; we have to consider whether we wish our people to remain a separate Jewish nation or whether we wish it to be broken up and dispersed. The nation will perish and the people be scattered if we let this man alone and do not put him to death. This argument decided the matter, and the Orthodox agreed that Jesus must be put to death; and they instructed the people to seize him as soon as he appeared in Jerusalem.

Though he knew of this, Jesus nevertheless went to Jerusalem for the feast of the Passover. His pupils entreated him not to go, but he said: What the Orthodox wish to do to me, and all that any man may do, cannot alter the truth for me. If I see the light I know where I am and where I am going. Only he who does not know the truth can fear anything or doubt anything. Only he who does not see, stumbles. And he went to Jerusalem, stopping on the way at Bethany. There Mary emptied a jar of precious oil on him, and when the pupils reproached her for wasting so much precious oil, Jesus, knowing that his bodily death was near at hand, said that what she had done was a preparation for his burial. When he left Bethany and went to Jerusalem, crowds met and followed him, and this convinced the Orthodox still more of the need to kill him. They only wanted an opportunity to seize him. He knew that the least indiscreet word from him now, contrary to the law, would be used as a reason for his execution; but notwithstanding this he went into the temple and again declared that the Jewish worship of God with sacrifices and libations was false, and he again announced his teaching. But his teaching, based on the prophets, was such that the Orthodox could still find no palpable breach of this law for which they could condemn him to death, especially as most of the common people were on his side. But at the feast there were certain heathen who having heard of Jesus's teaching, wished to discuss it with him. The pupils hearing of this were alarmed. They feared lest Jesus by talking with the heathen might betray himself and excite the people. At first they did not want to put the heathen in touch with Jesus, but afterwards they decided to tell him that these men wished to speak with him. On hearing this, Jesus was troubled. He understood that his talk with the heathen would make clear his rejection of the whole Jewish law, would turn the crowd from him, and would give occasion to the Orthodox to accuse him of having intercourse with the hated heathen; and knowing this he was troubled. But he also knew that his mission was to make clear to men, the sons of one Father, their unity without distinction of faith. He knew that to do this would cost him his bodily life but that its loss would give men a true understanding of life, and therefore he said: As a grain of wheat perishes to bear fruit, so I, a man, must give up my bodily life in order to bear spiritual fruit. He who holds fast to his bodily life loses his true life, but he who does not grudge his bodily life obtains the true life. I am troubled at what awaits me, but I have lived till now only in preparation for this hour, how then can I fail to act as I ought? So let the Father's will be manifested through me now.

And turning to the people, heathen and Jews, Jesus declared openly what he had only said privately to Nicodemus. He said: Men's lives, with their different creeds and governments, must all be changed. All human authorities must disappear. It is only necessary to understand the nature of man as a son of the Father of life, and this understanding destroys all divisions of men and of authorities and makes all men one. The Jews said: You are destroying our whole creed. Our law tells of a Christ, but you speak only of a Son of Man and say that he should be exalted What does that mean? He replied: To exalt the son of man means living by the light of understanding that exists in man, and while there is light, living by that light. I teach no new faith but only what each man may know within himself. Each man knows the life in himself, and each man knows that life is given to him and to all men by the Father of life. My teaching is only that man should love the life that the Father gives to us all.

Many of the unofficial folk believed Jesus; but the notables and official classes did not believe him, because they did not wish to consider the universal purport of what he said, and thought only of its temporal bearings. They saw that he turned the people from them and they wished to kill him; but they feared to take him openly, and wanted to do so secretly - not in Jerusalem and in the daytime. And one of his twelve pupils, Judas Iscariot, came to them, and they bribed him to take their emissaries to Jesus when he should be away from the people. Judas promised to do this, and went back to Jesus, awaiting a suitable opportunity to betray him On the first day of' the feast Jesus kept the Passover with his pupils, and Judas, thinking that Jesus was not aware of his treachery, was with them. But Jesus knew that Judas had sold him, and as they all sat at table he took bread, broke it into twelve pieces, and gave one to each of the pupils, to Judas as well as to the others, and without naming anyone, said: Take, eat my body. Then he took a cup with wine, gave it to them all, including Judas, to drink, and said: One of you will shed my blood. Drink my blood. Then he rose and washed all the pupils' feet, and when he had done so said: I know that one of you will betray me to death and will shed my blood, but I have fed him and given him drink and washed his feet. I have done this to show you how to behave to those who harm you. If you act so, you will be blessed. And the pupils all asked which of them was the betrayer. But Jesus did not name him, that they might not turn on him. When it grew dark, however, Jesus indicated Judas and at the same time told him to go away, and Judas got up from the table and went off and no one hindered him. Then Jesus said: This is what it means to exalt the son of man. To exalt the son of man is to be as kind as the Father not only to those who love us but to all men, even to those who do us harm. Therefore do not argue about my teaching, do not pick it to pieces as the Orthodox do, but do as I do and as I have now done before your eyes. This one commandment I give you: love men. My whole teaching is to love men always and to the end . After this, fear came over Jesus, and he went in the dark with his pupils to a garden to be out of the way. And on the road he said to them: You are all of you wavering and timid; if they come to take me you will all run away. To this Peter replied: No, I will never desert you and will defend you even to the death. And the other pupils all said the same.

Then Jesus said: If that is so, then prepare for defense, get weapons to defend yourselves and collect your provisions, for we shall have to hide. The pupils replied that they had two knives. When Jesus heard the mention of knives, anguish came over him. And going to a lonely spot he began to pray and urged the pupils to do the same, but they did not understand him. Jesus said: My Father - the spirit! End in me this struggle with temptation. Confirm me in the fulfillment of Thy will. I want to overcome my own wish to defend my bodily life, and to do Thy will - not resisting evil. The pupils still did not understand. And he said to them: Do not consider the body, but try to exalt the spirit in yourselves; strength is in the spirit, but the flesh is weak. And again he said: My Father! If suffering must be, then let it come: but in the suffering I want one thing only, that not my will, but Thine, may be fulfilled in me. The pupils did not understand. And again he strove with temptation and at last overcame it; and coming to his pupils he said: Now it is decided, you can be at rest. I shall not fight, but shall give myself up into the hands of the men of this world.

XI: THE FAREWELL DISCOURSE

And Jesus, feeling himself prepared for death, went to give himself up, but Peter stopped him and asked where he was going. Jesus replied: I am going where you cannot go. I am ready for death, but you are not yet ready for it. Peter said: I am ready to give my life for you now. Jesus replied: A man cannot pledge himself to anything. And he said to all his pupils: I know that death awaits me, but I believe in the life of the Father and therefore do not fear it. Do not be disturbed at my death, but believe in the true God and Father of life, and then my death will not seem dreadful to you. If I am united to the Father of life, then I cannot be deprived of life. It is true that I do not tell you what or where my life after death will be, but I point out to you the way to true life. My teaching does not tell you what that life is to be, but it reveals the only true path to that life, which is to be in unity with the Father. The Father is the source of life. My teaching is that man should live in the will of the Father and fulfill His will for the life and welfare of all men. Your teacher when I am gone will be your knowledge of the truth. In fulfilling my teaching you will always feel that you are in the truth and you in the Father. That the Father is in you. And knowing the Father of life in yourselves, you will experience a peace nothing can deprive you of. And therefore if you know the truth and live in it, neither my death nor your own can alarm you.

Men think of themselves as separate beings, each with his own separate will to live, but that is only an illusion. The only true life is that which recognizes the Father's will as the source of life. My teaching reveals this oneness of life, and presents life not as separate growths but as one tree on which all the branches grow. Only he lives who lives in the Father's will like a branch on its parent tree: he who wishes to live by his own will dies like a branch that has been torn away. The Father gave me life to do good, and I have taught you to live to do good. If you fulfill my commandments you will be blessed, and the commandment which sums up my whole teaching is simply that all men should love one another. And love is to sacrifice the bodily life for the sake of another:

there is no other definition. And in fulfilling my law of love you will not fulfill it like slaves who obey their master's orders without understanding them; but you will live as free men like myself, for I have made clear to you the purpose of life flowing from a knowledge of the Father of life. You have received my teaching not because you accidentally chose it, but because it is the only truth by which men are made free.

The teaching of the world is that men should do evil to one another, but my teaching is that they should love one another. Therefore the world will hate you as it has hated me. The world does not understand my teaching and therefore will persecute you and do you harm, thinking to serve God by so doing. Do not be surprised at this, but understand that it must be so. The world, not understanding the true God, must persecute you, but you must affirm the truth.

You are distressed at their killing me, but they kill me for declaring the truth, and my death is necessary for the confirmation of the truth. My death, at which I do not recede from the truth will strengthen you, and you will understand what is false and what is true and what results from a knowledge of falsehood and of truth. You will understand that it is falsehood for men to believe in the bodily life and not in the life of the spirit, and that truth consists in unity with the Father from which results the victory of the spirit over the flesh.

When I am no longer with you in the bodily life, my spirit will be with you; but like all men you will not always feel within you the strength of the spirit. Sometimes you will weaken and lose the strength of the spirit and fall into temptation, and sometimes you will again awaken to the true life. Hours of bondage to the flesh will come upon you, but only for a time; you will suffer and be again restored to the spirit as a woman suffers in childbirth and then feels joy that she has brought a human being into the world. You will experience the same when after being enslaved by the body you again rise in spirit, and feel such joy that there will be nothing more for you to desire. Know this in advance: in despite of persecution, of inward struggle and depression of spirit, the spirit lives within you and the one true God is the knowledge of the Father's will that I have revealed.

And addressing the Father, the spirit, Jesus said: I have done what Thou commandedst me, and have revealed to men that Thou art the source of all things, and they have understood me. I have taught them that they all come from one source of infinite life and that therefore they are all one, and that as the Father is in me and I am in the Father, so they, too, are one with me and the Father. I have revealed to them also that as Thou in love hast sent them into the world, they too should serve the world by love.

XII: THE VICTORY OF THE SPIRIT OVER MATTER

When Jesus had finished speaking to his pupils, he rose and, instead of running away or defending himself, went to meet Judas who was bringing soldiers to take him. Jesus went to him and asked him why he had come. But Judas did not answer and a crowd of soldiers came round Jesus. Peter rushed to defend him and, drawing a knife, began to fight. But Jesus stopped him and told him to give up the knife, saying that he who fights with a knife himself perishes by a knife. Then he said to those who had come to take him: I have till now gone about among you alone without fear, and I feel no fear now, I give myself up to you to do with me as you please. And all his pupils ran away and deserted him.

Then the officer of the soldiers ordered Jesus to be bound and taken to Annas, a former high priest who lived in the same house as Caiaphas, who was high priest that year and who had devised the pretext upon which it was decided to kill Jesus: namely, that if he were not killed the whole nation would perish. Jesus, feeling himself in the will of the Father, was ready for death and did not resist when they took him, and was not afraid when they led him away; but that very Peter who had just assured Jesus that he would rather die than renounce him, the same Peter who had tried to defend Jesus, now when he saw Jesus being led to execution was afraid they would execute him too, and when the door-keeper asked whether he had not been with Jesus, denied him and deserted him.

Only later, when the cock crowed, did Peter understand all that Jesus had said to him. He understood that there are two temptations of the flesh - fear and strife - and that Jesus had resisted these when he prayed in the garden and asked the pupils to pray. And now he, Peter, had yielded to both these temptations against which Jesus had warned him: he had tried to resist evil and to defend the truth had been ready to fight and do evil himself; and now in fear of bodily suffering he had renounced his master. Jesus had not yielded either to the temptation to fight when the pupils had two knives ready for his defense, or to the temptation of fear - first before the people in Jerusalem when the heathen wished to speak to him, and now before the soldiers when they bound him and led him to trial.

Jesus was brought before Caiaphas, who began to question him about his teaching. But knowing that Caiaphas asked not to find out about his teaching but only to convict him, Jesus did not reply, but said: I have concealed nothing and conceal nothing now: if you wish to know what my teaching is, ask those who heard it and understood it. For this answer the high priest's servant struck Jesus on the cheek. Jesus asked why he struck him, but the man did not answer him and the high priest continued the trial. Witnesses were brought and gave evidence that Jesus had boasted that he would destroy the Jewish faith. And the high priest questioned Jesus, but seeing that they did not ask in order to learn anything, but only to pretend that it was a just trial, he answered nothing.

Then the high priest asked him: Tell me, are you Christ, a son of God? Jesus said: Yes, I am Christ, a son of God; and now in torturing me you will see how the son of man resembles God.

The high priest was glad to hear these words and said to the other ͵judges: Are not these words enough to condemn him? And the judges said: They are enough: we sentence him to death. And when they said this, the people threw themselves upon Jesus and began to strike him, to spit in his face, and to insult him. He remained silent.

The Jews had not the right to put anyone to death: to do this permission was needed from the Roman governor. So having condemned Jesus in their court, and having subjected him to ignominy, they took him to the Roman governor Pilate that he might order his execution. Pilate asked why they wished to put Jesus to death, and they answered that he was a criminal. Pilate said that if that was so, they should judge him by their own law. They answered: We want you to put him to death, because he is guilty before the Roman Caesar: he is a rebel, he agitates the people, forbids them to pay taxes to Caesar, and calls himself the King of the Jews. Pilate called Jesus before him, and said: What is the meaning of this - are you King of the Jews? Jesus said: Do you really wish to know what my kingdom is, or are you only asking me for form's sake? Pilate answered: I am not a Jew, and it is the same to me whether you call yourself King of the Jews or not, but I ask you who you are and why do they call you a king? Jesus replied: They say truly that I call myself a king. I am indeed a king, but my kingdom is not an earthly one, it is a heavenly one. Earthly kings have armies and go to war and fight, but as you see they have bound and beaten me and I did not resist. I am a heavenly king and my power is in the spirit.

Pilate said: So it is true that you consider yourself a king? Jesus replied: You know it yourself. Everyone who lives by the spirit is free. I live by this alone, and teach only to show men the truth that they are free if they live by the spirit. Pilate said: You teach the truth, but nobody knows what truth is. Everyone has his own truth. And having said this he turned away from Jesus and went back again to the Jews, and said: I find nothing criminal in this man. Why do you wish me to put him to death? The chief priests said: He ought to be executed because he stirs up the people. Then Pilate began to examine Jesus before the chief priests, but Jesus, seeing that this was only for form's sake, answered nothing. Then Pilate said: I alone cannot condemn him. Take him to Herod.

At the trial before Herod, Jesus again did not answer the chief priests' accusations, and Herod, taking Jesus to be an empty fellow, mockingly ordered him to be dressed in a red cloak and sent back to Pilate. Pilate pitied Jesus and began to persuade the chief priests to forgive him, if only on account of the feast;

but they held to their demand, and they all, and the people with them, cried out to have Jesus crucified. Pilate again tried to persuade them to let Jesus go, but the priests and the people cried out that he must be executed. They said: He is guilty of calling himself a son of God. Pilate again called Jesus to him, and asked. What does it mean that you call yourself a son of God? Who are you? Jesus answered nothing. Then Pilate said: How is it that you do not answer me, when I have the power to execute you or to set you free? Jesus replied: You have no power over me. All power is from above. And Pilate for the third time tried to persuade the Jews to set Jesus free, but they said to him: If you will not execute this man whom we have denounced as a rebel against Caesar, then you yourself are not a friend to Caesar, but a foe. And on hearing these words Pilate gave way and ordered the execution of Jesus. But they first stripped Jesus and flogged him, and then dressed him again in the red cloak. And they beat him and insulted him and mocked him. Then they gave him a cross to carry and led him to the place of execution, and there they nailed him to the cross, and as he hung on the cross the people all mocked at him. And to this mockery Jesus answered: Father, do not punish them for this, they do not know what they are doing. And later, when he was already near to death, he said: My Father! Into Thy care I yield my spirit. And bowing his head he breathed his last.

finis

From: *What I Believe* (1885)

They told me we must believe and pray.

But I felt I had little faith, and therefore could not pray. They told me one must pray God to give faith - the very faith that gives the prayer that gives the faith that gives the prayer - and so on to infinity.

But both reason and experience showed me that only my efforts to fulfill Christ's teaching could be effective.

And so, after many, many vain seekings and studyings of what was written in proof and disproof of the Divinity of this teaching, and after many doubts and much suffering, I was again left alone with my heart and the mysterious book. I could not give it the meaning others gave it, could not find any other meaning for it, and could not reject it. And only after disbelieving equally all the explanations of the learned critics and all the explanations of the learned theologians, and after rejecting them all (in accord with Christ's words, 'Except ye turn and become as little children, ye shall in no wise enter into the kingdom of heaven'), I suddenly understood what I had not formerly understood. I understood it not as a result of some artificial, recondite transposition, harmonization, or reinterpretation; on the contrary, everything revealed itself to me because I forgot all the interpretations. The passage which served me as key to the whole was Matt. v. 38, 39: 'Ye have heard that it was said, An eye for an eye and a tooth for a tooth: But I say unto you, Resist not him that is evil.' And suddenly, for the first time, I understood this verse simply and directly. I understood that Christ says just what he says, and what immediately happened was not that something new revealed itself, but that everything that obscured the truth fell away, and the truth arose before me in its full meaning. '*Ye have heard that it was said, An eye for an eye and a tooth for a tooth: But I say unto you, Resist not him that is evil.*' These words suddenly appeared to me as something quite new, as if I had never read them before. Previously when reading that passage I had always, by some strange blindness, omitted the words, 'But I say unto you, Resist not him that is evil', just as if those words had not been there, or as if they had no definite meaning.

Subsequently, in my talks with many and many Christians familiar with the Gospels, I often had occasion to note the same blindness as to those words. No one remembered them, and often when speaking about that passage Christians referred to the Gospels to verify the fact that the words were really there. In the same way I had missed those words and had begun understanding the passage only from the words which follow, 'But whosoever smiteth thee on thy right check, turn to him the other also. . .' and so forth; and these words always appeared to me to be a demand to endure sufferings and deprivations that are unnatural to man. The words touched me, and I felt that it would be admirable to act up to them; but I also felt that I should never be strong enough to fulfill them merely in order to suffer. I said to myself, 'Very well, I will turn the other cheek, and I shall again be struck. I will give what is demanded and everything will be taken from me. I shall have no life - but life was given me, so why should I be deprived of it? It cannot be that Christ demands it.' That was what I formerly said to myself, imagining that in these words Christ extolled sufferings and deprivations, and extolling them, spoke with exaggeration and therefore inexactly and obscurely.

But now, when I had understood the words about not resisting him that is evil, it became plain to me that Christ was not exaggerating nor demanding any suffering for the sake of suffering, but was only very definitely and clearly saying what he said. He says: 'Do not resist him that is evil, and while doing this know in advance that you may meet people who, having struck you on one cheek and not met with resistance, will strike you on the other, and having taken away your coat will take your cloak also; who, having availed themselves of your work, will oblige you to do more work, and will not repay what they borrow ... should this be so, continue nevertheless to abstain from resisting the evil man. Continue, in spite of all this, to do good to those who will beat you and insult you.'

And when I understood these words as they are said, at once all that was obscure became clear, and what had seemed exaggerated became quite exact. I understood for the first time that the center of gravity of the whole thought lies in the words, 'Resist not him that is evil', and that what follows is only an explanation of that first proposition. I understood that Christ does not command us to present the cheek and to give up the cloak in order to suffer, but commands us not to resist him that is evil, and adds that this may involve having to suffer. It is just like a father sending his son off on a distant voyage, who does not order the son not to sleep at night and not to eat enough, and to be drenched and to freeze, but says to him, 'Go your road, and if you have to be drenched and to freeze, continue your journey nevertheless'. Christ does not say, offer your cloak and suffer', but he says, 'Resist not him that is evil, and no matter what befalls you do not resist him'. These words, 'Resist not evil', or 'Resist not him that is evil', understood in their direct meaning, were for me truly a key opening everything else, and it became surprising to me that I could so radically have misunderstood the clear and definite words: 'It was said, An eye for an eye and a tooth for a tooth: But I say unto you, Resist not him that is evil, and no matter what he does to You, Suffer and surrender, but resist him not.' What can be clearer, more intelligible, and more indubitable than that?

And I only needed to understand these words simply and directly as they were said and at once Christ's whole teaching, not only in the Sermon on the Mount but in the whole of the Gospels, everything that had been confused, became intelligible; what had been contradictory became harmonious, and, above all, what had appeared superfluous became essential. All merged into one whole, and one thing indubitably confirmed another like the pieces of a broken statue when they are replaced in their true position. In this Sermon and in the whole of the Gospels everything confirmed the same teaching of non-resistance to evil. In this Sermon, as everywhere else, Christ never represents his disciples - that is to say, the people who fulfill the law of non-resistance to evil otherwise than as turning the cheek to the smiter, giving up the cloak, persecuted, beaten, and destitute. Everywhere Christ repeatedly says that only he can be his disciple who takes up his cross and abandons everything; that is to say, only he who is ready to endure all consequences that result from the fulfillment of the law of non-resistance to evil. To his disciples Christ says: 'Be beggars; be ready without resisting evil to accept persecution, suffering, and death.' He himself prepares for suffering and death without resisting evil, and sends Peter away because he complains of this. He himself dies forbidding resistance to evil, and without deviating from his teaching. All his first disciples fulfilled this commandment of nonresistance, and passed their lives in poverty and persecutions, never returning evil for evil.

So Christ says what he says. It is possible to affirm that it is very difficult always to obey this rule. It is possible not to agree with the statement that every man will be happy if he obeys this rule. It may be said that it is stupid, as unbelievers say that Christ was a dreamer and an idealist who enunciated impracticable rules which his disciples followed stupidly. But it is quite impossible not to admit that Christ said very clearly and definitely just what he meant to say, namely that according to his teaching man should not resist evil, and that therefore whoever accepts his teaching must not resist evil. And yet neither believers nor unbelievers understand this simple, clear meaning of Christ's words.

AZILOTH ||| BOOKS

Aziloth Books publishes a wide range of titles ranging from hard-to-find esoteric books - Parchment Books - to classic works on fiction, politics and philosophy - Cathedral Classics. Our newest venture is Aziloth Books Children's Classics, with vibrant new covers and Black-and-White/Colour illustrations to complement some of the world's very best children's tales. All our imprints are offered to the reader at a competitive price and through as many mediums and outlets as possible.

We are committed to excellent book production and strive, whenever possible, to add value to our titles with original images, maps and author introductions. With the premium on space in most modern dwellings, we also endeavour - within the limits of good book design - to make our products as slender as possible, allowing more books to be fitted into a given bookshelf area.

We are a small, approachable company and would love to hear any of your comments and suggestions on our plans, products, or indeed on absolutely anything. We look forward to meeting you.

Contact us at: info@azilothbooks.com.

PARCHMENT BOOKS enshrines the concept of the oneness of all true religious traditions - that "the light shines from many different lanterns". Our list below offers titles from both eastern and western spiritual traditions, including Christian, Judaic, Islamic, Daoist, Hindu and Buddhist mystical texts, as well as books on alchemy, hermeticism, paganism, etc..

By bringing together such spiritual texts, we hope to make esoteric and occult knowledge more readily available to those ready to receive it. We do not publish grimoires or any titles pertaining to the left hand path. Titles include:

Abandonment to Divine Providence	Jean-Pierre de Caussade
Corpus Hermeticum	G.R.S. Mead (trans.)
The Holy Rule of St Benedict	St. Benedict of Nursia
Kundalini	G. S. Arundale
The Way of Perfection	St. Teresa of Avila
Q.B.L.	Frater Achad
The Cloud Upon the Sanctuary	Karl von Eckhartshausen
The Confession of St Patrick	St. Patrick
Nightmare Tales; The Voice of the Silence	H. P. Blavatsky
The Outline of Sanity	G K Chesterton
The Teachings of Zoroaster	Shapuji A Kapadia
The Dialogue Of St Catherine Of Siena	St. Catherine of Siena
Esoteric Christianity	Annie Besant
The Wisdom of the Egyptians	Brian Brown
The Spiritual Exercises of St. Ignatius	St. Ignatius of Loyola
Dark Night of the Soul	St. John of the Cross
Moses and Monotheism	Sigmund Freud
Man, His True Nature & Ministry	Louis-Claude de St.-Martin
The Gospel of Thomas	Anonymous
Alchemy Rediscovered and Restored	Archibald Cockren
The Imitation of Christ	Thomas à Kempis
The Interior Castle	St. Teresa of Avila
Songs of Innocence & Experience	William Blake
De Rerum Natura	Lucretius
The Secret of the Rosary	St. Louis de Montfort
Tertium Organum	P. D. Ouspensky
From Ritual to Romance	Jessie L. Weston
De Anima (Concerning the Soul)	Aristotle
Njal's Saga	Anonymous

Obtainable at all good online and local bookstores.
View Aziloth Books' full list at: www.azilothbooks.com

CATHEDRAL CLASSICS hosts an array of classic literature, from erudite ancient tomes to avant-garde, twentieth-century masterpieces, all of which deserve a place in your home. All the world's great novelists are here, Jane Austen, Dickens, Conrad, Arthur Machen and Henry James, brushing shoulders with such disparate luminaries as Sun Tzu, Marcus Aurelius, Kipling, Friedrich Nietzsche, Machiavelli, and Omar Khayam. A small selection is detailed below:

The Prophet	Kahlil Gibran
Herland	Charlotte Perkins Gilman
With Her in Ourland	Charlotte Perkins Gilman
Frankenstein	Mary Shelley
The Time Machine; The Invisible Man	H. G. Wells
Three Men in a Boat	Jerome K Jerome
The Rubaiyat of Omar Khayyam	Omar Khayyam
A Study in Scarlet	Arthur Conan Doyle
The Picture of Dorian Gray	Oscar Wilde
Flatland	Edwin A. Abbott
The Coming Race	Bulwer Lytton
The Adventures of Sherlock Holmes	Arthur Conan Doyle
The Great God Pan	Arthur Machen
Beyond Good and Evil	Friedrich Nietzsche
England, My England	D. H. Lawrence
The Castle of Otranto	Horace Walpole
Self-Reliance, & Other Essays (series1&2)	Ralph W. Emmerson
The Art of War	Sun Tzu
A Shepherd's Life	W. H. Hudson
The Double	Fyodor Dostoyevsky
To the Lighthouse; Mrs Dalloway	Virginia Woolf
The Sorrows of Young Werther	Johann W. Goethe
Leaves of Grass - 1855 edition	Walt Whitman
Analects	Confucius
Beowulf	Anonymous
Agnes Grey	Anne Bronte
Plain Tales From The Hills	Rudyard Kipling
The Subjection of Women	John Stuart Mill
Silas Marner	George Eliot
The Rights of Man	Thomas Paine
Progress and Poverty	Henry George

Obtainable at all good online and local bookstores.
View Aziloth Books' full list at: www.azilothbooks.com

AZILOTH CHILDREN'S CLASSICS Aziloth Books is passionate about bringing the very best in children's classics fiction to the next generation of book-lovers. Renowned for its original design and outstanding quality, our highly successful list has something to suit every age and interest. Titles include:

The Railway Children	Edith Nesbit
5 Children and It	Edith Nesbit
Anne of Green Gables	Lucy Maud Montgomery
What Katy Did	Susan Coolidge
What Katy Did Next	Susan Coolidge
Puck of Pook's Hill	Rudyard Kipling
The Jungle Books	Rudyard Kipling
Just So Stories	Rudyard Kipling
Alice Through the Looking Glass	Charles Dodgson
Alice's Adventures in Wonderland	Charles Dodgson
Black Beauty	Anna Sewell
The War of the Worlds	H. G Wells
The Time Machine	H. G .Wells
The Sleeper Awakes	H. G. Wells
The Invisible Man	H. G. Wells
The Lost World	Sir Arthur Conan Doyle
A Christmas Carol	Charles Dickens
Call of the Wild	Jack London
Greenmantle	John Buchan
Treasure Island	Robert Louis Stevenson
Dr Jekyll and Mr Hyde	Robert Louis Stevenson
Gulliver's Travels	Jonathan Swift
Catriona (David Balfour)	Robert Louis Stevenson
The Water Babies	Charles Kingsley
The First Men in the Moon	Jules Verne
The Secret Garden	Frances Hodgson Burnett
A Little Princess	Frances Hodgson Burnett
Peter Pan	J. M. Barrie
The Song of Hiawatha	Henry W Longfellow

Obtainable at all good online and local bookstores.
View Aziloth Books' full list at: www.azilothbooks.com